# A Filly Called Easter

## By

## Laura Hesse

Running L Productions
Nanaimo, B.C.

# A Filly Called Easter

National Library of Canada Cataloguing in Publication Data
Hesse, Laura - 1959
    A Filly Called Easter/by Laura Hesse

    ISBN: 0-9734013-2-X


    1. Ponies-Juvenile Fiction. 2. Easter/Seasonal stories. Canadian (English) 1. Title.

Publisher/Distributor
#9 - 2993 104th Street
Nanaimo, BC
Canada V9T 2E6
Email: RunningL@bcsupernet.com
www: runninglproductions.com

Printed in Canada

*To Mom...My Inspiration...Break a Leg and All That Jazz!*

Other books by Laura Hesse

## The Holiday Series:

### One Frosty Christmas

Published December 2003
Running L Productions
ISBN: 0-9734013-0-3

### The Great Pumpkin Ride

Published September 2004
Running L Productions
ISBN: 0-9734013-1-1

### A Filly Called Easter

Published March 2005
Running L Productions
ISBN: 0-9734013-2-X

# Acknowledgments

To all my readers...your gracious phone calls and emails have spurred me on to complete The Holiday Series. Your support has been truly amazing. Read. Write. Learn. Thanks also to my editor, Dianne Andrews, cover layout specialist, Linda Hildebrand of Phantom Press, and the print specialists at Friesen's. Thanks also to Robin (aka, Easter) and Morna Caplan for assisting me with the cover photo shoot. A special thank you to Jacque Duncan of At The River's Edge Stables and Bettina Bobsien, DVM, for their medical expertise and advise on pregnant horses. May all your mounts be swift and your mountains an easy climb.

My thanks,


*Laura L. Hesse*

# Contents

# Chapter One

## *The Auction*

"Dad?" Linda McCloud asked casually from across the kitchen table, a spoonful of Cheerios in one hand, the bowl on the table in front of her more cereal than milk.

"Yes, Sweet Pea," Tom McCloud replied. He sighed heavily and put down the Financial Post, a dispirited look on his face. Beef prices were still low and showed no sign of getting any better. He folded the paper an extra two times and tossed it in the recycle box by the door: out of sight, out of mind!

"Can I come to the auction with you and Ross today?" his daughter beamed sweetly.

Tom looked up and grinned, his spirits lifting at the sight of the sparkling blue eyes and the earnest face that greeted him. Linda was the image of her mother: blue-grey eyes, shoulder length dirty blond hair and a full moon face. She was the picture of innocence, however cheeky her motive. His heart swelled with pride whenever he looked at her. His daughter never ceased to amaze

1

him and he wasn't surprised by her question. Tom tried to keep his face stern and sober. He already knew why she wanted to come today, but didn't let on.

"You don't think that you'd be bored? Cattle auctions, these days, aren't much fun," he said, lifting a mug to his lips. He gulped down the last of the strong coffee and placed the "World's Greatest Dad" mug down on the table. It had been a Christmas present from his son and daughter a couple of years ago; it was his favorite cup.

"I won't get in your way. I promise. I'd just like to go, that's all," she finished. "You've never taken me before and I wanna see the bulls. I think it'd be neat!"

"Well, I guess we can spare the seat-space. What do you think, Ross?"

Ross looked up from his bacon and eggs. He stuffed a piece of toast into an egg yolk and squished it all around. "S'okay with me," he said, then stuffed the dripping toast into his mouth.

Linda grinned. She knew she could rely on her big brother for support. He was four years older than she was and always looked after her. They didn't fight much because Ross was either too busy or not at home. When he wasn't doing his own farm chores, he was helping his girlfriend, Jenny Weatherspoon, at the Running L Riding Academy with hers.

Tom pushed his chair away from the table and stood up. "Well, you kids finish your breakfast while I hook up the stock trailer. I don't know if we'll come home with anything. This isn't the best time to be lookin' at buyin' a new bull, but you never know, do you, Sweet Pea?"

"Nope! You never know," Linda agreed.

Her father chuckled, grabbed his coat from the coat hook by the kitchen door and headed outside. A cold blast of air swept through the kitchen in his wake, ruffling Linda's hair.

"That was smooth, Lindy," Ross mouthed through a mouthful of eggs. "Does this have anything to do with Albert's tellin' you that there's goin' to be a horse sale too?"

Linda shrugged and gobbled down the last of her Cheerios.

Ross laughed. He shook his head and pushed away from the table. "I suppose it's time that we retired old Sally. You're getting too big for her anyway." He added amiably, "That mare's gotta be 35 by now."

"You won't tell Dad, will you?" Linda looked up.

Ross chuckled. "No. If you see anything that you like, come get me and I'll have a quick look. If I like what I see, I'll go and fetch Dad," Ross nodded. "If there's nothin' at the auction, then I'll talk to Jenny. There might be some horses for sale at the Running L."

"Thanks, bro," she said.

Ross slipped on his jacket and threw Linda's cardigan at her. She dived across the table and snatched it out of the air before it landed across Ross' dirty plate.

"Rossss," she moaned.

Ross burst out laughing as he pulled open the door. He looked outside, then turned to Linda. "Come on. Dad's waiting," he said, leaving the door ajar behind him.

Linda quickly tugged on the sweater and her gumboots. She could feel the cold and clammy rubber right through her woolen socks. Linda skipped through the

3

doorway and let the wind slam the door shut behind her. Her mother and Waffles, the new family dog, were shopping in town so there was no one to yell or to bark at her for it. Waffles couldn't be left alone yet or he would eat his way through furniture, doors, socks, pillows; basically, he would eat whatever was of interest at the time.

Linda jumped into the truck and sat sandwiched between her father and her brother on the front seat of her father's Ford F350. They turned left on the highway and headed for Cold River. From there, they would go north on County Road No. Ten until they reached Knob Hill. The largest auction house in the district was in Knob Hill as well as three slaughterhouses. Linda didn't like to think about the slaughterhouses. She knew many of her favorite cows ended up there. Her family were ranchers; that was just the way it was.

She stared vacantly out of the truck's windows watching the myriad of farms roll by. The rumbling hum of the Ford's big diesel engine filled her ears. The men didn't talk much so she contented herself by playing 'I-spy' inside her head.

I-spy something that is blue, she thought to herself.

A blue sign appeared in the distance. It said a campsite and a boat launch were coming up: Take Exit 53.

Linda watched Exit 53 pass them by.

She sighed, giving up on the game. It wasn't much fun to play alone anyway so she turned her thoughts to the auction and prayed that she would find a horse that she liked there. She loved Sal, her Norwegian Fjord mare, but Sal was just a pony...and a fat pony, to boot! Linda was eleven now and really wanted a chance at winning

4

the barrel races at the next Harvest Feast. That gave her almost eight months to find a new horse and to train it.

Linda gazed out the window. The fields were still partially snow-covered; the sloughs filled with water and slush, the ground too wet and too muddy to prepare for spring planting for at least another two months. It would be six weeks before the earth was firm enough to support a tractor. Cattle stood in mud up to their knees in many farm yards, their coats dirty and ragged from the long winter.

The sun was dazzlingly bright; it reflected off the puddles and slick pavement, blinding those traveling along the highway. The road was a patchwork quilt of dried white salt and wet rivulets of spring run-off. The snow banks along the highway's shoulder were small blackened mounds of ice, gravel and dirt.

The sign for Knob Hill came up quickly.

Linda's father turned right off the highway. Gravel shot out from under the truck's winter tires as it bumped over the washboard surface that was County Road No. Six. Three miles further along, they saw the long, low tin roofed buildings and white railed stockyards that were Knob Hill Auctions. The muddy parking lot was filled with dual axle trucks and rusty stock trailers. Tom McCloud pulled his Ford in alongside all the rest.

"Well, let's see what we can see," Tom drawled as the truck rolled to a stop. He smiled half-heartedly at his son and daughter.

Linda fidgeted in her seat, anxious to be checking out the stock pens.

Tom opened up his door, got out and stretched his lean and lanky frame. Linda undid her seatbelt and slid across the seat, after her father. Ross jumped out on the far side and slammed the truck's door shut.

Tom put a hand on his daughter's shoulder. "You stay clear of the bull pens. I don't want you near any of those bulls, you hear? You can sit up in the stands with us and look at them from there."

Linda nodded, her eyes wide. "I won't! I don't want to get stomped on!"

Tom roared with laughter. "I don't want you to get stomped on either."

The three McClouds walked into the auction house together. Several men called out a greeting to Tom. He waved and answered back. The rank smell of mud and cattle filled the air; it was as sour as an old outhouse. The bulls honked and roared. Some slammed themselves against their metal pens as men with electric prods in their hands hustled down the aisles, yelling and driving the bulls into the holding pens outside the sales ring. Others stood inside their muddy pens, stupidly staring off into the distance and mindlessly chewing on hay.

Tom left the kids outside and went into a small white trailer where he registered and picked up his bidding number.

"Where do you think the horses are?" Linda whispered to her brother, hopping from one foot to the other. She skidded sideways in the mud. Ross grabbed her by the arm and steadied her.

"The auction ring is over to the left. There's a row of bench seats above it. That's where Dad and I will be. The bulls are mostly in the outside pens and will be brought in by number so I expect the horses are through that door to the right."

6

"Can I go look or should I wait for Dad?" Linda asked, a hopeful look on her face.

"Wait for Dad," Ross advised.

Tom walked over to the kids, stuffing his buyer's number inside his coat pocket. "Well, I've bin told that there's a couple of real dandy Limousin bulls here and a few Black Angus that might be of interest to us," he said to Ross. "We'll take a walk out back and take a look at 'em before headin' into the sales ring."

Ross nodded.

"Dad? There's a horse sale too. Can I go look?" Linda jumped up and down on the spot, her eyes shining.

"Is there now?" Tom winked at Linda. "I hadn't heard about that."

Linda slapped Ross across the arm.

"I didn't tell him!"

Tom McCloud laughed heartily. "Ease off, little girl. I already knew about it. I suspected that was why you wanted to come."

"You did?"

"Yes, I did!"

The three of them stood and laughed together. The auctioneer's voice boomed over the loud speaker, the words rolling off his tongue. "Five! Five! Who'll give me five-fifty?"

"Go on. Go look at the horses, but be careful. Don't get in any of the wrangler's way. I'm sure you'll find us if you need to," Tom said.

Linda squealed with delight and ran for the horse pens, her father and brother watching until she disappeared through the barn's door.

7

Linda scooted around a tall pile of hay bales, then skidded to a stop. There were dozens of wooden railed pens filled with scrawny, mangy cattle and horses. The sharp overhead lights made every rib stand out. Men with downcast faces and eyes wandered about the pens, their shoulders slumped in defeat. Slim boys in stained jeans and gumboots forked hay into the pens. The cattle and horses kicked and bit their neighbors, fighting for the feed. Tears filled Linda's eyes. It was clear that many ranchers had tried to hold out through the winter but hadn't made it...the sad eyes and racks of ribs was the result!

She slowly walked by the pens of thin cattle and thanked God that they had two really good cuttings of hay last year. Her mother complained that her father was a Scrooge, but now Linda was grateful for it.

She kept her eyes to the ground until she rounded the corner and reached the first of the horse pens. She stopped and looked over the stall door. Six rangy mustangs looked at her, their eyes filled with mistrust, their mouths filled with hay. She reached over the gate and tried to scratch a dark bay filly with a half-moon on her forehead, but the horse spooked backwards and almost toppled over a big bay gelding.

"You won't do. You're way too spooky," Linda said sadly.

She moved on to the next pen. A chubby, white Welsh pony nickered and stretched his head out to her. He was fat and rolly-polly, just like Sal. She laughed and tickled him behind the ears. The pony tipped his head sideways and leaned into her hand, loving the attention.

8

A young, raven haired woman wandered towards her, stopped and leaned against the stall door.

"He's cute, isn't he?" she said. She giggled as the pony lifted his head and nibbled on her coat sleeve, clearly wanting her to pet him too.

"He is. He's a lot like my pony, Sal," Linda replied.

"I'm looking for a pony for my daughter. She's only five. He'd be a good size for her. All the other horses and ponies that I've seen are much too big and some are quite wild," the woman volunteered.

"I bet this little guy would suit you. He's really friendly, but he needs to go on a diet." Linda laughed.

"I don't know much about horses. A friend suggested that I come and look at the auction," the woman said. "I just don't know what I'm looking at and I'd be terrified to go into the ring and bid on him. I'm afraid that I'd get carried away and pay too much."

"I can have my dad or my brother have a good look at him, if you want? Dad knows a lot about horses. He'll tell you if he thinks this pony is sound," Linda offered. "You have to watch ponies; most of them are easy-keepers and can founder. My dad can tell you if he thinks he's foundered before. You shouldn't buy him if my father says not to, even if you really like him. We have to watch old Sally too. She's a real pig and will eat until she bursts!"

"Thank you, I'd appreciate that," the woman replied. "I had no idea that there was that much to it."

"I'm trying to find a horse for myself. It's time for us to retire Sal," Linda added as she moved down to the next pen, the woman walking along beside her.

9

"There's a really pretty horse over there," she pointed. "Turn left at the end of this aisle and go to the very
back of the building. There is a very pretty yellow and
white horse there...I don't know what they call her...I really don't know very much about horses, I'm afraid...but
she seems really out-of-place here. She's very friendly,
not like the rest of them at all."

"I'll go and look." Linda thanked the woman and ran
down the alley. She glanced at the horses in the pens she
passed, but none of the horses seemed worth a second
look. She dodged a chap with a wheelbarrow, clipped
him on the elbow and muttered an apology. She raced on
until she found her way to the horse in question.

The filly popped her head over top of the stall door
and whinnied at Linda. Linda skidded to a stop, her eyes
widening and her mouth falling open at the sight of the
dark palomino before her. The filly's eyes were big and
round; they regarded her with a calm intelligence. She
had a white blaze down the middle of her face and a luxurious white mane and tail.

"Wow! You're beautiful!" Linda exclaimed.

Linda stroked the filly's nose. The horse snorted,
dipped her head back inside her stall, then lifted it back
up, her mouth filled with hay. She nuzzled Linda's hand
gently, then reached over the door and looked down the
aisle, fascinated by all the hubbub going on around her.

Linda leaned closer and looked the filly over. Her
belly was distended; the filly was obviously very pregnant. She was strikingly colored: her coat was dark yellow and she had four white socks that stretched almost to
the top of her legs. She was well muscled, despite the fat
stomach. Linda thought she was the prettiest horse that

she had ever seen. All thoughts of a barrel racer were swept from her mind.

There was a hand-written sign tacked to the stall door that read: "Hello, my name is Easter because that's the day that I was born two years ago. My mom passed away recently and my dad didn't know what to do with me so here I am. Please take me home!"

"Easter...is that you, girl?" Linda whispered to the filly. The little filly snorted and snuggled closer to Linda. Linda laughed. "I'm going to run and get my dad and my brother. Hang on, Easter. I want you to kick anybody if they try and take you away, okay?"

The filly snorted and moved away, as if in understanding. She stuck her nuzzle deep inside the pile of hay just inside the stall door and worked her way to the bottom of the pile to where the best pieces lay.

Linda bolted down the aisle, arms pumping, gumboots flapping. Horses and cattle scurried back from their stall doors. The loudspeakers crackled overhead as more cattle were auctioned off. Bulls trumpeted from the outside pens. Men hollered and pushed them into the sales ring. Linda burst through the door into the sales area.

"Dad!" she cried breathlessly, hurdling the rows of benches two at a time.

"Linda, slow down!" her father scolded from his seat in the center of the bleachers.

Several men shook their heads and wagged a finger at Linda as she danced by them.

"Oh, sorry," Linda apologized after knocking a rancher's coffee to the floor. The rancher shook his head and muttered something under his breath. Linda ignored

11

him and slid her fanny along the bench, sidling in close to her father. "Dad, you have to come and see Easter."

"See who?" Ross muttered, his eyes on the gigantic Limousin bull that was just being led into the ring. He elbowed his father gently; this was one of the bulls they were interested in.

"Easter!" Linda almost shouted.

"Linda, settle down," her father commanded, his eyes narrowing in annoyance.

"Dad. You have to come and meet Easter. She's only two, but that's okay. She's pregnant, but that's okay too! She is the prettiest horse that I've ever seen. She makes Pizzazz look like puppy chow," Linda said furiously, knowing that would get a response from Ross, if not her father.

"Pizzazz isn't puppy chow," Ross replied angrily, turning in his seat and glaring at his little sister.

"She is beside Easter!" Linda smirked, hiding her glee. Now she had her father's attention.

"Let me get this straight. You found a two year-old pregnant filly named Easter that you want me to buy for you?" Tom asked, his eyebrows raised in disbelief. "I thought you wanted a barrel racer?"

"Yep and yep! Oh, I forgot, there's this really nice lady who wants to buy a pony for her daughter and there is a really cute Welsh pony back there, but she doesn't know anything about ponies so I told her that you would help." Linda added, "The pony's even fatter than Sal so I told her that you would take a good look at him and that she shouldn't buy him if you say not too. Okay?"

She tugged on her father's arm. "Come on, Dad, pll-lleeeaaassse...," she wailed.

12

Tom McCloud sighed and shook his head.

"Let's go, son. We shouldn't be spending any money right now anyway. Scratch, our old bull, will do for another year. Maybe next year we'll replace him." Tom stood up and made his way down the row of seats. He looked at the bull in the ring, shook his head at the owner, the man that he had talked to in the back pens, and walked out of the sales arena. His son followed along behind him, a disgruntled look on his face. Ross had wanted that bull and was more than a little angry with his sister for taking them away from the bidding.

"Some folks are really having some bad times here," Tom commented as he wandered past the cattle and horse pens. "Best thing is to slaughter them, I guess." His eyes grew sad as he realized that if his luck had been worse, these could have been his cows!

Linda pulled her father by the hand until they reached the little palomino filly's stall. The palomino poked her head out of the stall and whinnied at Linda. Linda threw herself at the horse, wrapping her arms around her neck. The filly stood calmly as Linda hugged her tightly and cooed into her ear.

Tom read the sign tacked to the stall. Ross stood beside him.

"Well, let's have a good look at her," Tom said, opening the stall door.

The three of them ambled into the stall. The filly moved aside to let them in and stood quietly nuzzling Linda's hands.

"Well, I have to agree with sis, Dad. This is a nice little filly. She sure doesn't belong here," Ross scratched his

13

head. "It's obvious her owner doesn't realize what kind of an auction that he's brought her to!"

"What worries me is that she's pregnant. She's too young to be bred. Don't know what silly fool let that happen. She's got a lot of growin' to do still." Tom bent down and picked up a hoof; the filly willingly gave it to him. He gently placed the hoof back on the ground and gave the horse a gentle pat. She sniffed his hand and moved in closer to Linda. "She sure likes you, Sweet Pea, but you won't be riding her for at least a year, you know that?"

Linda nodded. She bit her lip and held her breath, hoping that her father would let her bid on the palomino.

"You'll have to ride Sal for another year. I expect this girl will be foalin' sometime in the next six weeks," her father said as he ran a hand over the filly's belly. "You're gonna have your hands full with her. She'll need training and I expect you to learn how to do it. The foal will have to be dealt with too and God knows what kinda foal it's gonna be."

"I'll learn whatever I have to, Dad. Please can we bid on her?" Linda pleaded.

"Well," her father said, rubbing his chin.

Linda could see by the brooding look on her father's face that he wasn't convinced in the least to buy Easter. His frown deepened and Linda choked back her tears. She looked at Ross, her eyes pleading for help.

"She's a nice mare, Dad," Ross said, winking encouragement at his little sister, his anger forgotten. "She's flashy, but Pizzazz isn't no puppy chow!"

Linda grinned. "It made you come see Easter, didn't it?"

Ross and her father crowed with laughter. The filly snorted and danced backwards.

A man in cleanly pressed jeans and a bright blue ski-jacket stopped by outside the stall door. His leather shoes were ruined; the brown leather was covered in mud and manure. He looked as out-of-place as the filly called "Easter" did.

"Do you like her?" he asked, nervously. He had a slight tick above one eye that made him look even more skittish than he was.

"I love her," Linda piped up.

"You own the filly?" Tom asked, feeling sorry for the man standing there. The old fellow looked tired and worn-out; he had much the same look as a lot of the ranchers that wandered in and out of the stock pens, only his clothes were finer.

"She belonged to my late wife," he said.

Tom smiled slightly, feeling awkward, not sure what to say.

"It's okay. Dad's gonna buy her for me, aren't you?" Linda said, sweetly.

"Might be, Sweet Pea, but we'll have to see what happens in the ring," her father cautioned.

"I put a reserve bid on her of two thousand dollars," the man said.

Tom and Ross burst out laughing.

"Good on you, sir," Ross said.

A flicker of a smile crossed the man's lips. "I didn't want her to go for meat or to go to just anyone. I prayed that some good folks like yourselves would come by and see our Easter," he said. "I'm forgetting myself. My name is Will Sims. This, as you know, is Easter."

Tom extended a hand and the men shook hands. Tom introduced his family.

Linda curtsied, deciding that she better be on her best behavior.

"Don't get too carried away, Lindy," Ross cautioned, his eyes twinkling with mirth.

"The lady at the office recommended that I put a reserve on Easter to make sure nothing bad happens and I'm glad I listened to her. She told me that I could pull her out at any time, but if I sold her privately that I had to pay the auctioneers ten percent."

"Yep, that's standard," Tom said. "How about you and I go and get a coffee and discuss what you want for little Easter here, Mr. Sims? I don't expect that there's anyone here willing to pay that price right now."

"Please, call me Will. That's not necessary. I'd gladly give her to the right person and I think that your daughter will do quite nicely."

"No way," Linda yelped. Getting Easter for free would be a dream come true. There was no way that she thought her father would argue with that.

"We can't take her for nothin', Will. That wouldn't be right," Tom said.

Linda held her breath, her heart skipping a beat, knowing the matter wasn't settled yet. She clamped a hand over her mouth and closed her eyes, praying that her father would give in. She didn't want to say anything that might make him change his mind. Her father talking to Mr. Sims was one thing, agreeing on a price and being able to take Easter home with them was quite another.

"Then, how about I withdraw her from the auction and you come home with Easter and me for a cup of tea and we'll negotiate from there," Will offered.

Tom smiled and placed a reassuring hand on his daughter's shoulder. "Now that's an offer that none of us will turn down."

Easter whinnied and nodded her head.

Everyone burst out laughing.

"We have to find the nice lady that told me about her, Dad. I promised that you'd look at that Welsh pony," Linda said, earnestly.

Mr. Sims smiled, his face almost cracking with the effort.

"Now I know that I've found the right young lady for Easter."

Just then, a tall woman with a puzzled look on her face rounded the corner and waved at Linda. Linda waved back.

"That's her, Dad!"

"Alright," Tom said, shaking his head in confusion. "Let's go look at that pony. It seems that it's horses that everyone wants today, not bulls." He looked down at his daughter. "And I suppose if she buys the pony, we're gonna be trailering it to her house for her too?"

Linda smiled sweetly.

"Yep, that's what I thought." Tom grinned and walked towards the nervous woman.

"I don't think Dad is gonna bring you to anymore auctions, Lindy," Ross whispered.

Linda shrugged and cuddled up beside Easter. The filly playfully nipped at Linda's hair. Mr. Sims chuckled and haltered the palomino.

17

"How about you come with me while your dad is helping that young woman out and we'll go load Easter back into my trailer?" Mr. Sims said to Linda.

"Okay!" Linda chirped.

Ross snorted back a laugh and followed after his father, leaving his sister to look after her new horse. He wondered what his girlfriend would say when he told her about Easter. He guessed that she'd probably fall in love with the filly when she saw her too; Easter kinda had that effect on people. Ross chuckled. He suspected his mother's reaction might be a little different; his father and sister were going to have some serious explaining to do when they got home.

# Chapter Two

*Easter*

"Are we gonna be able to find our way back to the highway?" Ross asked, looking out the window as his father followed along behind Mr. Sims' white truck and trailer. Mr. Sims' headlights flashed; he stopped and made another right turn.

"Yeah, I think so," his father replied, not sounding too sure of himself.

They bounced over yet another gravel road, the fifth turn since leaving the main highway. This section of Knob Hill was well-treed and the roads winding; the farms were small hobby farm type properties, not the big spreads like farther south.

The Welsh pony in the back whinnied and kicked the sides of the trailer. The woman, Sherry Arneson, was thrilled at having bought the pony for $100 with Tom McCloud's help. The pony was well behaved in the auction ring and under saddle with Linda on top of him. When the local ranchers saw Tom bidding on the pony with a pretty woman sitting beside him, kneading her hands together and looking terrified whenever someone else bid, they all elbowed each other and teased Tom that they were going to find a phone and call his wife. The two other bidders, both meat buyers, lowered their bidding cards and waved at Tom. Sherry had no idea what was going on around her and broke into a loud cheer when the auctioneer told Tom that they had just bought themselves Christmas dinner if the pony didn't work out. The ranchers had all howled with laughter, slapping their knees and cheering. It was the bright spot in a very hard day for many of them.

It seemed the only problem with the little fellow was that he didn't like to travel. After trying to coax the pony into the trailer for forty minutes using every trick available including a bucket of oats and a bag of carrots, Tom and Ross finally got behind him and lifted him into the stock trailer butt first while Linda pulled him forward with the lead rope. This brought on another round of cheers from a gang of wranglers who had gathered around to watch the little white pony get the best of the whole McCloud family.

Mr. Sims turned left and drove up a tree-lined driveway, his truck bumping its way slowly up a gravel path between two stone gates with black wrought-iron horses atop the posts. Easter poked her nose out the side window of the trailer and snorted. She turned her head and looked back at the vehicle traveling behind her.

"Dad! She's looking right at me!" Linda squealed.

"Yeah, I think she is, Sweet Pea," her father agreed.

Ross grinned and elbowed his sister in the ribs.

20

The lane ended abruptly. It circled around in front of a large, two-storey stone house with a cobbled front entrance and shuttered windows. The yard was neat and tidy, the cedar and yew hedges trimmed and square. Two iron lamp posts marked the entry to the front porch, illuminating a thick oak door with a fabulous stained glass window featuring a rearing black unicorn. The side yard was cobblestone too. It looked like an English country manor house, out of place, yet oddly fashionable set as it was amidst a grove of poplars. Gently sloping pastures fell away to the north and north-east.

"Wow!" Ross exclaimed. "I'm guessing Mr. Sims doesn't want for much. No wonder he offered Easter to us for nothing."

"I'll hear no more of that!" Tom McCloud ordered. "We'll pay a fair price for the filly."

Ross saw his father's jaw set in that stubborn look that meant it was not a time to argue with him. He raised an eyebrow at Linda. She stayed quiet on the seat beside him, not wanting to try her father's patience any further.

They pulled up in front of the house, careful to leave enough space behind the trailer for Mr. Sims to unload Easter. The filly nickered; the pony answered in kind. Mr. Sims got out of his truck and made his way towards the Ford, his shoulders slumped, his gait uneven.

"We can put the pony in the barn with Easter while we have a cup of tea," Mr. Sims said to Tom through the side window.

"Sounds like a good idea. I just hope we can get that little devil back in the trailer," Tom said, then chuckled. "He's creating quite an up-roar." Tom gave his daughter a piercing look.

Linda shrugged and grinned.

"I'll get him," Ross offered.

"I'll get Easter," Linda piped.

"Uh, huh," Tom agreed.

They all got out of the truck and opened the doors on both trailers, Tom looking after Mr. Sims as it was clear the old man was very tired.

Ross led the pony out of the open-sided stock trailer. The white pony squealed and reared. Ross gave one sharp tug on the lead line and the pony stopped misbehaving. He arched his head and grunted when Linda unloaded Easter, then tried to bolt and run towards the filly. Despite being close to six feet tall, Ross had a hard time hanging onto the little fellow. The Welsh pony dragged him across the cobblestones by his boot heels, not stopping until he was nose to nose with the palomino filly.

Easter snorted and stretched out her head, sniffing the unknown visitor. She squealed, a high pitched sound that hurt the ears, and flicked her tail, then raised a rear leg in warning. The pony snorted and backed off.

"Well, I guess Easter's straightened him out." Tom laughed.

"I think he's in love," Linda said.

"The barn is around the back. There's lots of hay so help yourself to what you need. You'll see the path to the back door. It leads to the kitchen," Mr. Sims advised.

Ross and Linda nodded, then walked off with Easter and the pony in tow. They were a comical sight: the slick, blond, very pregnant mare, waddling along beside the white, even wider, stubby-legged pony. The pony was better behaved now that he had company.

The kids stabled and fed the horses, then made their way up the back porch steps and kicked their muddy boots off at the landing. They stepped with stocking feet into the kitchen, their nostrils flaring and their mouths watering at the divine smell of cinnamon and coffee that permeated the room.

Ross whistled under his breath.

The kitchen was immense! It had grey granite counter tops and floors, maple cabinets with polished copper pots hanging on hooks underneath, and a great big iron woodstove with a rock chimney. The stove and chimney took up the whole of one wall. A fire raged inside the open doors of the woodstove, filling the room with a cozy yellow light, and warming the granite floors. The kitchen table was oak. It was surrounded by deep, luxurious captains' chairs that invited one to sit and rest. Hand-knit rag carpets adorned the floors, bringing color and warmth into the room.

Ross was glad that his mother wasn't with them or they'd never get home.

Mrs. Worthing, a plump woman with grey hair and perpetual laugh lines etched into her dimpled face, fussed about the stove. Her face was red and sweaty; she was clearly bewildered by the on-set of all these guests, appearing as they did, without warning. Mr. Sims tut-tutted and consoled her, informing his housekeeper that she was about to meet Easter's new owner and wasn't that alone worth all the fuss? Mrs. Worthing chattered to herself nonstop. She whipped up a plateful of cinnamon buns and oatmeal raisin cookies, hot from the oven, as if she had known that visitors were coming all along.

23

"Mrs. Worthing has been a godsend," Mr. Sims said, his eyes growing misty. "I don't know what I would have done without her after Pearl got so sick. She has been chief cook, housekeeper, nurse and good friend, ever since."

Mrs. Worthing fairly flew across the kitchen after Mr. Sims' kind words, her cheeks flushed with pleasure and her eyes sparkling. She held a plate of goodies and a pot of hot coffee in her hands which she deposited on the table with a flourish, then was off to the china cupboard in one quick motion. With a smile on her face, she took the fine china down from the cupboard and placed the dainty tea-cups and saucers on the table in front of each of the guests. She bustled back to the table and placed a pot of steaming tea down beside the coffee urn.

The McClouds looked from one to the other, not sure of how to proceed. Linda had never seen china so pretty and dainty. Tom worried that he'd break the handle off one of the cups, his hands too big and too calloused for such finery. Ross by-passed the cups and grabbed Linda's arm, nodding towards the wash basin and towels by the door.

The kids went and washed up, then sat down at the kitchen table with their father and Mr. Sims. Linda couldn't wait to dive into the cookies.

"So you're the one wot will be takin' our girl, Easter?" Mrs. Worthing asked merrily with a broad Yorkshire accent, her eyes bright and quick.

"Yes," Linda chirped through a mouthful of cookie. "She's the prettiest filly that I've ever seen and I love her already."

Mrs. Worthing snorted in amusement.

"And Easter is quite taken with young Miss McCloud," Mr. Sims added.

"You'll have ta tell 'em the story of Easter then," Mrs. Worthing nodded. "Tis truly amazing, 'cept for the part about that rogue next door, Mr. Morris. It's 'is fault that our Easter is in the heavenly-way." Mrs. Worthing scowled; a comical look as her face and character weren't used to such harsh thoughts.

"Now, now, Mrs. Worthing. T'wasn't his fault exactly. That stallion of his is young and untrained," Mr. Sims consoled her.

Having none of it, Mrs. Worthing muttered, "Right, then he oughtn't ta own one, should he?"

Mr. Sims sighed, a weary sound, as if he'd been through this argument a hundred times already.

"What kind of stud has he got then?" Tom asked. He took a sip of coffee, preferring java to tea, despite Mrs. Worthing's frown and raised eyebrows. "Mighty fine coffee, ma'am."

Mrs. Worthing flushed, happy with the praise, despite her thinking all north Americans mad for wanting coffee in the afternoon instead of good English tea.

"These are the best cookies that I've ever tasted," Linda mumbled. "They're even better than my mom's, but I won't tell her that."

Ross nodded and kept eating, snapping up a second cinnamon bun.

"He's breeding Spanish Mustangs. They're a rangy lot that he picked up from somewhere in the States. I don't know much about the breed myself. He's got a young blue roan stallion that is quite ill mannered, I dare say, but I suppose that's to be expected. Mr. Morris wants to re-introduce the mustangs to the wild...some project of his," Mr. Sims shook his head, his face a mask of confusion. "I suspect the poor breeder that sold them to him hadn't a clue about what he was going to do."

"He lets 'em all run havoc, he does," confided Mrs. Worthing.

"I don't quite understand what he expects to accomplish myself," Mr. Sims added.

"Accomplish? He's daft, thas wot he is!" Mrs. Worthing announced, wiping her hands on her apron.

Linda and Ross giggled.

"Sounds like he is," Tom agreed. "There's no call for that anymore. There's only a few places left in all of North America that horses can run wild and they're managed pretty carefully."

Mrs. Worthing beamed down at him and filled his coffee cup back up.

"Mr. Morris is a biologist. He says he's testing some theories about herd instincts and how man has changed the herding instincts of domestic horses. It seems to me that he should be studying truly wild horses rather than doing what he's doing. Makes no sense at all," Mr. Sims pondered.

"Right! The man has no sense. Daft! Didn't I just say it?" Mrs. Worthing moaned.

"So how did Easter get pregnant?" Linda asked innocently.

"Well. Do you remember that fierce storm we had here last year?" queried Mr. Sims.

"That was a bad one," Tom agreed, twiddling a spoon in his coffee cup.

26

"Morris' stallion broke down my fencing during the night and led his herd into the hills on the other side of my property. I didn't know they were there..." Mr. Sims said, but Mrs. Worthing cut him off.

"And of course, the bloke next door couldn't be bothered ta ring us up and tell us, could he?" she said, stiffly.

Ross caught his sister's gaze and rolled his eyes at Linda. Linda elbowed him back.

"Yes. Right." Mr. Sims paused. "Well then, I let Easter out into her paddock when the weather settled down a bit. I heard this awful commotion and turned around in time to see Easter galloping off across the meadows with a herd of Spanish Mustangs. My wife was in the final stages of cancer and took a turn for the worse when she saw Easter running off with that young stallion. We had to rush her to the hospital in Edmonton. I didn't get back home to retrieve Easter for several days."

"Good Lord, that's terrible," Tom said, dropping his spoon.

"Aye, that's wot I says," Mrs. Worthing muttered, liking Tom McCloud even more. Mrs. Worthing would never forget Mrs. Sims' cries of anguish at the sight of Easter disappearing over the ridge with that gang of ruffians, nor would she forget the sight of her mistress collapsing in a heap on the floor afterwards. It was the shock that did it.

"I dare say that I haven't spoken much to Mr. Morris ever since," confessed Mr. Sims.

There was silence at the table. Mr. Sims seemed to drift off, his eyes vacant as if he were somewhere else for the moment. Mrs. Worthing fussed about, but stilled her tongue.

27

"Was Easter born here?" Linda asked, changing the subject.

Mr. Sims shook himself like a dog shaking water from his coat after a swim in the river. "Why, yes, she was."

"Easter's ma was Mrs. Sims' darling." Mrs. Worthing stopped cleaning the counter for a moment and smiled.

"Aye, she was a lovely old mare. Easter has her nature; gentle and true. She was a very pretty palomino, just like Easter, but she was quite old when she gave birth. My wife couldn't bear not to have a foal out of her. It was a miracle that Easter survived; the mare had a terrible go of it and we almost lost her a couple of times. Along came our little filly, feisty and tough, but sweet as pie."

"Now that's the wee version...tell 'em the whole tale, Mr. Sims. It's a right wonder, it is," offered Mrs. Worthing.

"I suspect that you'd tell it better than I so why don't you have a go," Mr. Sims said kindly.

"Ooooh, I'd love ta," Mrs. Worthing blushed. "Well 'ere goes then."

Mrs. Worthing poured herself a cup of tea, added a thin slice of lemon to it, and sat down at the table.

"It was a right gawd-awful night, raining so hard that you couldn't see yer hand in front of yer face. Cats and dogs, it was. I was in the kitchen gettin' ma hot cross buns ready for the mornin so's I just had to pop 'em in the oven, then we'd be off to Easter Service. Mrs. Sims, against the doctor's orders, mind you, put on her coat and rubbers and told me she was goin' out ta the barn ta check on old Ester. Ester of course was Easter's ma. Well, the wind grew wickeder and wickeder. I put on a pot of hot tea, knowing that Mrs. Sims was goin' ta need some fortifying when she got back, then finished kneading ma dough. I realized that Mrs. Sims hadn't come back and called the Master ta tell 'im where she was, ya see? I tried ta talk her outa it, I tol 'im, but she wouldn'a listen.

Mr. Sims and I both went out through that drivin' rain. I never got so wet'n all ma life as runnin' across the yard that night. When we got ta the barn, we found Mrs. Sims crying over Ester. The mare was a sight. She was wet and steamy like a balmy summer's day, poor thing. Anyways, Mr. Sims orders me ta go an fetch the vet so I runs back ta the house, but the phones are out 'cause a the storm. It near broke ma heart ta 'ave ta tell Mr. and Mrs. Sims that I couldn'a get through ta the doctor.

Mr. Sims knew what ta do though so he says to me, 'Mrs. Worthing, bring me some towels, soap and hot water. I think I know wot's wrong.' I runs back ta the house, then back ta the barn again. I must'a looked like a drowned kitten ma'self by the time I done all that runnin'.

Mr. Sims feels old Ester's belly and inspects her, just like the vet would. He says, 'The foal's breeched'. Well, I knew right then as wot was the problem. The poor wee'un was turned the wrong way round.

Mr. Sims washes his hands real good and doesn't he go in ta poor old Ester and turn the foal the right way round. Course he didn't tell us until long afterwards that he hadn't a clue wot he was doing. 'Read it in a book once,' he says ta us over a cup a tea one day. Old Ester, she just lays there all quiet with Mrs. Sims stroking her cheek and shivering at her head, caring more fer that old

horse than she did fer 'erself. Mrs. Sims she keeps talkin'
ta Ester, keepin' her calm. It made ma heart swell, it did."
Mrs. Worthing dabbed at the corner of her eyes with the
tip of her apron. Mr. Sims reached over and patted her
hands, tears forming in his eyes too.

"Anyway, that old mare knew wot ta do, she did. She
heaved and pushed, gruntin' like a ripe old sow until her
bairn popped out all slick and pretty as can be. We all
cheered when we saw the foal was a pretty palomino just
like her ma. Just then, the wind shook the barn so hard, I
thought it was goin' ta fall down on us. That's when we
noticed that the wee thing wasn't breathing. She just lay
in the straw, her eyes closed and her body all wet and
still. Mr. Sims gets down on his knees right away and
cleans out the filly's mouth, then starts blowin' inta her
nose, but that doesn't work either so he starts pumpin'
the little one's chest an breathin' inta her nose again. We
figured the poor thing was done fer. Gone to see God
already is wot we all thought. All at once, the filly kicks
out and takes a deep breath. I just about had a heart
attack waitin' for that wee thing ta decide it wanted ta
stay in this world.

Of course, we found out from the vet that it's common fer folks that don't know much about foalin' ta think
the foals up'n died. Lots of 'em like ta lay there for
awhiles after they've bin born and catch their breath so ta
speak. Mr. Sims didn'a have ta blow in her nose and
pound on her chest like he did. We all had quite a good
laugh over it, didn't we?"

"Humm," Mr. Sims cleared his throat and raised an
eyebrow.

Mrs. Worthing ignored him and carried on.

"Ester knew she'd done herself proud; she struggled ta her feet and stood there, all shivery and sweaty like she'd just run across the country. Mrs. Sims threw a blanket over her ta keep her from gettin' too cold. That filly coughed and struggled ta get ta her feet, but just didn'a have the strength. Mr. Sims, he gets in there and tries ta help. The wee bairn nipped his fingers and wouldn'a let 'im, had ta do it herself, ya see? I expect she was still mad at 'im fer pounding on her like he did. Took her some time, but finally she gets up, all wobbly on those spindly little legs of hers, but she manages. Ester lowered her head and gave the foal a little nudge and the little 'un started ta suck right away.

Mrs. Sims started ta cry and said, 'It's a miracle. Something told me that I had ta check on Ester. It's a good thing I listened. Wot would have happened, Will, if I hadn'a listened?'

Well, that's when Mrs. Sims decided that the little filly had ta be named, 'Easter'. A miracle is wot it was; an Easter miracle."

Mrs. Worthing drew a deep breath, then added, "An that's the story of our Easter."

"Wow," Linda muttered, her eyes wide, the half-eaten cookie on her plate all but forgotten.

"What happened to the old mare?" asked Ross.

"She passed away a few days after my wife. I found her in her stall one morning, laying quietly on the ground, her head tucked down. She looked very peaceful; almost like she was resting. The straw wasn't even disturbed. The vet said he thought she had a heart attack. I like to think Ester and my wife are together now. Easter went into quite a funk when the old mare died, wouldn't

31

eat for a couple of days; that's when I decided that I needed to find her a good home. I'm too old to start training horses again and I don't have the heart with Pearl gone," Mr. Sims said sadly, his shoulders shaking.

"Easter will have a good home with us, Mr. Sims, and you can come visit anytime," volunteered Linda.

"That's a fact," her father said. "You're both more than welcome to come stay at the farm and visit for as long as you want."

"Ooh, my! That's mighty fine, Mr. McCloud," fussed Mrs. Worthing, wiping away a long trail of tears from her face.

"Call me Tom, please," Tom said.

"You'll definitely have to come an see the foal when it arrives," added Ross. "It'll be interesting to see what kinda color that she's gonna throw. I'll bet she throws a grulla colt."

"No way. I want another pretty palomino filly, just like her mother and her grandmother," argued Linda.

Tom, Will Sims and Mrs. Worthing burst out laughing.

"Well, you can put your order in, Sweet Pea, but it ain't up to you," Tom said, pushing himself away from the table. "That was a wonderful treat, but we better get moving. We have to drop that little imp of a pony off at Sherry's place in Cold River before we head home. You kids go and load the filly and pony up while I settle with Mr. Sims."

"Yes, sir," Ross and Linda agreed, standing up.

Linda wrapped her arms around Mrs. Worthing's ample waist and gave her a big hug. Mrs. Worthing blushed a deep crimson and cuddled her back.

"You'll do right fine by our Easter, I'll warrant," Mrs. Worthing cooed. Linda laughed and gave her another hug.

Ross shook hands with Mr. Sims and headed out the back door.

"A right fine family you have there, Tom," Mr. Sims said.

"Yes. They're good kids," Toms answered proudly.

# Chapter Three

## The Long Ride Home

Linda walked Easter up the ramp into the trailer; the filly waddled into the large stock trailer as if she hadn't a care in the world. The pony screamed and pawed at the earth, his right front hoof scraping on the cobblestoned lane. Ross had a terrible time holding onto him. The little fellow couldn't stand to be parted from the palomino; unlike at the auction, this time he couldn't wait to get inside the trailer with Easter!

"Have ya got Easter tied yet, Lindy?" yelled Ross, the pony tucking his head down and dragging him across the driveway. "This little devil is strong!"

The pony reared and landed with a thump, his front hooves clattering on the ramp. Easter turned her head, a mouthful of timothy waggling up and down as she happily helped herself to the feedbag tied to the side of the trailer, a look of amusement on her face. The pony whinnied, a high pitched frantic scream. Easter ignored him and turned her attention back to the feed in front of her.

34

Linda chuckled and skipped down the ramp. "Okay, Ross," she said with a wink.

Ross groaned and gave a sharp tug on the pony's lead line, trying to make him pay attention. He stepped onto the ramp and steadied himself, knowing the pony would try to bolt into the trailer. The Welsh didn't disappoint him!

The pony charged up the ramp. Ross yanked hard on the lead line. The pony finally gave his head to the pressure and pranced his way the rest of the way into the trailer beside Ross. Ross shook his head and tied the pony next to the filly, then gave Easter a reassuring pat.

"Don't worry, girl, it won't be long and you'll be rid of him," he said. Easter snorted in agreement. Ross burst out laughing and gave her another pat before rechecking the lead ropes to make sure both were secure. He refilled the pony's feedbag and leapt out of the trailer, then lifted up the ramp and slid the bolts into place.

"Right, you kids ready?" their father asked as he stepped out onto the front porch with Mr. Sims and Mrs. Worthing following closely behind him.

"Yep," chirped Linda.

"All ready," Ross agreed.

Mr. Sims' face was pale and his hands shook with tremors. It was clear that Easter's leaving was breaking his heart. Ross offered his hand to Mr. Sims and they shook hands in farewell.

Linda threw herself at the old man and wrapped her arms around his thin waist, her face beaming. "Don't be sad, Mr. Sims. We aren't that far away!"

"Bless yer heart, child," Mrs. Worthing cried.

Mr. Sims chuckled and hugged the young girl to his chest, his rheumy eyes brightening.

"You're right, dear. You're not," he agreed.

"I expect you'll have a call when we get home," Tom McCloud said with a shake of his head. His daughter never ceased to amaze him. "We will also expect you and Mrs. Worthing to come for Sunday dinner next week and I won't take 'No' for an answer. We're easy to find. Just head east on the main highway towards River Bend. Our spread is about 3 miles this side of town. Number 3460 is on the blue mailbox at the end of the drive. The farmhouse is a white two storey with a big front porch."

Mr. Sims mouth fell open. Speechless, he nodded a reply. Mrs. Worthing placed a steadying hand on his shoulder.

"Away we go, kids," Tom ordered.

Ross and Linda quickly jumped into the truck. Tom fired up the old diesel and headed down the lane in a puff of blue smoke. Linda leaned over her father and waved out the window as the truck pulled onto the road.

"Dad says come for about three o'clock!" she yelled.

Mr. Sims and Mrs. Worthing waved back, then stood on the porch watching until the Ford's tail-lights disappeared around the corner.

"I think y'ev done the right thing," Mrs. Worthing muttered.

"Aye," Mr. Sims said under his breath, "but it's left an awful emptiness."

"Not for long, I'll warrant." Mrs. Worthing smiled.

Mr. Sims chuckled, his thin shoulders trembling. "You think?"

"I know!" Mrs. Worthing stated, broaching no argument. "That family's done an adopted us without us evenin' knowing."

Mr. Sims snorted and turned around, then made his way back into the house. Mrs. Worthing stood on the porch for another moment, staring off into the distance. It was going to be difficult with Easter gone. There would be no more going down to the stable in the morning to feed the filly and no more wandering around at night worrying about her. The master was right in saying, "it's left an awful emptiness", but Mrs. Worthing would bet a year's salary that they hadn't seen the last of Easter nor little Linda McCloud!

"I like them!" Linda stated out loud.

"So do I," Ross agreed.

"I can see your mother and Mrs. Worthing putting their heads together and taking on all the women in the county at next year's Harvest Feast bake-off," Tom added.

The three of them chuckled.

"Yum," Linda said, rubbing her stomach.

"I can handle a few more of those cinnamon buns," stated Ross.

"How? You ate three! I thought I was going to have to ask Mrs. Worthing to adopt you as obviously we don't feed you enough at home," Tom joked, turning left onto the main highway.

Linda sat up straight, a big grin on her face. She couldn't wait to see what her mother and all her friends would think of Easter. She was sorry to take Easter away from Mr. Sims...he was such a sad man...and vowed that she would take extra special care of the filly so that Mr. Sims wouldn't be so sad anymore. It was so exciting; they were going to have a baby!

"I wonder what I should call her?" Linda said, squirming around in her seat.

"Call who, Sweet Pea?"

"Easter's baby."

"It might be a colt, you know?" Ross gave his sister a gentle shove.

"Nope. No way! I got a feeling that Easter's gonna have a filly," Linda retorted.

"Don't be naming it anything before it's born, Sweet Pea," Tom said, seriously. "It's bad luck! Easter's got a ways to go yet and she's mighty young to be foaling. I don't want to worry you, but we need to wait and see what happens."

Linda's eyes widened and filled with tears, her father's words frightening her.

"Dad's not tryin' to scare you, Lindy. You just have to be prepared," Ross consoled her.

"Ross is right. That filly's not half old enough to be pregnant. I'm surprised nature didn't take its course already and cause the filly to lose the foal." Tom gave his daughter a quick look, then turned his attention back to the road. He didn't like having to be so blunt, but his daughter needed to understand the facts. If it wasn't for Will Sims' situation, he probably wouldn't have agreed to buy the palomino, no matter how nice she was. Even now, he wondered if he had done the right thing. He could just imagine the look his wife was going to give him when he got home. He had refused to spend any money on a new garden shed for her, but he'd buy his daughter a new horse! Tom chuckled under his breath. He suspected that, whether he liked it or not, he was going to be buying a new shed tomorrow.

Icy, wet sleet began to fall from the sky. The clouds lowered; the horizon was dark and brooding. The tires squished and squelched on the wet tarmac. The cattle in the fields alongside the highway were huddled close to their barns.

Linda sat quietly on the front seat, staring out at the road as the sleet turned to thick white flakes of snow. She folded her hands in her lap and prayed quietly to herself. Ross put an arm across the seat back behind her; it was as close to a hug as he would give her in front of anyone.

"Please, God. Protect my Easter and her foal," Linda prayed to herself, her brows knitting tightly together. "You have to!"

The sign for Cold River passed them by. They turned west and watched for a blue double-wide mobile home with white shutters and an old red barn behind it. That was how Sherry described her place. She said that you couldn't miss it as the trailer was as blue as Lake Louise and you could see it from miles away.

"There it is," Ross said, pointing down the highway. "Wow, you sure can't miss it!"

They wheeled into the driveway. Sherry and her daughter, a smaller black haired and brown eyed version of her mother, waved from the living room window. The sight of the little girl jumping up and down and wringing her hands in excitement cheered Linda up. She agreed with Ross. She had never seen a house painted that bright a blue in all her life. It almost hurt the eyes to look at it.

The white pony fit right in, what with the bright white shutters and doors.

Tom pulled up to the barn. Ross and Linda jumped out of the truck and walked around back to the trailer. Easter snorted. The filly's forelock was tipped with snow. The pony nickered, his face hidden, his body too short for him to see out the slats in the sides of the trailer. He kicked the trailer for no apparent reason. Easter pinned back her ears and nipped the pony in the neck. It was clear that she'd be glad to be rid of him.

Ross lowered the trailer's ramp, then went inside and untied the pony just as Sherry's daughter came bolting out of the house and across the front yard, her jacket flapping around her waist. The pony whinnied at the little girl and pranced down the ramp with Ross holding tight to the lead shank.

"Mommie. He's so cute! Is he really mine?" the little girl's voice warbled, her eyes wide and bright.

"Yes, thanks to these kind folk," Sherry said, then smiled. "Thank you so much for all your help."

Tom blushed. "Thank my daughter."

"What's your name?" Linda asked from inside the trailer, her hand on Easter's neck to keep her quiet.

"Jen. What's yours?"

"Linda. This is my new horse," Linda said, stroking the palomino's neck. Easter nuzzled her shoulder.

"Ooooh, she's pretty," Jen said.

Linda beamed.

"How come she's so fat? She's even fatter than my new pony."

Linda burst out laughing.

"That's because Easter is gonna have a baby."

40

"Neat. Can I come see it when it's born?" Jen asked, her head tilted to one side and her eyes twinkling with innocence.

"Sure."

Tom McCloud grunted, realizing that he may as well give up. It seemed as if half the province would be coming down to their farm to see Easter's foal when it was born. He hoped that miracles happened twice! Privately, he didn't hold much hope for the foal, but the filly had already beaten all the odds so maybe her foal would too. This certainly wasn't the day that he had planned.

Seeing the frustration on her father's face, Linda left Easter alone and snuggled in close to her father. His face brightened and he smiled down at her.

"So have you thought up a name for that pony of yours?" he asked Jen.

Jen's face twisted into a stern mask. She grimaced and pursed her lips. "Snowflake!" she announced, squaring her small shoulders, as if daring anyone to say it was a silly name.

"That's a good one," Tom solemnly agreed.

Jen sighed with relief. She paused for a moment, then looked up at Tom. "Yep. I'm gonna call him Snowflake because it's snowin' right now and he's white!"

"What if it was snowin' and he was a black pony?" Linda asked, curious.

Jen's eyes lit up and she said in her very serious five year old voice, "Well, then I'd have to call him Stormy."

Everyone laughed.

"Well, how about you come with me and we'll go put Snowflake in the barn," Ross volunteered.

"Okay," Jen said, taking hold of Ross' free hand.

41

Sherry, Tom and Linda watched them go. The tall, handsome boy led the pony away with one hand while gently holding onto one of Jen's tiny hands with the other. He listened intently as she chattered away to him all the way to the barn. Every few steps, Snowflake would stop and cast a forlorn look at Easter.

Linda broke away from the adults and walked up the ramp into the trailer to check on her filly. Easter's eyes were shiny; she watched Linda's every move. The filly's face was dusted with snow, the top of her mane and her forelock were tipped with ice. Her chest was wet and sweaty, a thin layer of foam gathering there. Linda felt her sides. The palomino wasn't breathing heavy; that was a good sign. Linda's hand jumped an inch off the filly's belly. Linda yelped.

"What is it, Sweet Pea?" her father asked, turning quickly and walking up the ramp.

"The foal moved." Linda grinned, then patted Easter's neck. "Easter's really sweaty though, Dad. I think there's something wrong."

Her father moved in beside her and felt the filly's neck, then ran his hand down her chest, the insides of her legs and back along her belly.

"Humpf," he grunted.

"I have an old blanket in the barn that would probably fit her," Sherry offered.

"That might be a good idea. I don't like how the filly is sweating in this cold. We don't want her to catch a chill, do we, Sweet Pea? I just wasn't prepared to be bringin' back a pregnant horse." Tom grinned at his daughter, but the smile didn't reach his eyes.

Linda knew that her dad was worried about Easter. The stern look on his face made her realize how serious the horse's condition was. Suddenly, Linda was really scared. What if she lost both the filly and the foal? She closed her eyes and prayed harder. Easter reached her head around and nuzzled Linda's shoulder. Linda opened her eyes and leaned her head against the filly's neck.

"Let's get that blanket," Tom said. He and Sherry walked side-by-side, heading towards the barn, leaving Linda alone with Easter.

"It's gonna be okay, girl. I'll look after you, even if I have to sleep in the barn to keep an eye on you and the baby. Don't you worry," Linda whispered and hugged the filly.

The snow eased off as the temperature warmed and the wind picked up. The wind howled around the trailer. The snowflakes turned to sleet, then to hail which battered the top of the trailer, then to a driving rain. Linda shivered and tugged her collar up around her ears. The trailer rocked gently, buffeted by the wind.

Her father returned with a torn and faded green blanket. It had a worn, grey woolen lining. He threw it over Easter's back and fastened the front buckles. He pulled the belly band up and snapped it snugly over Easter's big belly. The filly let out a heavy sigh.

"Right, let's get her home," Tom suggested. "Thanks, Sherry."

"Well, that's the least I could do. Don't worry about returning the blanket."

Ross came back, Jennifer chirping away beside him. Ross looked amused. "Easter okay?" he asked.

"She's frettin' a bit. We need to get her stabled," his father replied.

With another quick goodbye, they wished Sherry, Jen and Snowflake well. Linda promised to phone Jen when Easter had delivered her foal. Ross pulled up the ramp and they were on their way home.

# Chapter Four

## *A Handful of Easter*

The McClouds pulled into their muddy yard, all three of them happy to be home. Waffles, their German Shepherd came charging out of his house, barking and wagging his tail. Easter poked her nose out of the trailer and nickered. Mary McCloud pushed open the back door and wandered out onto the porch.

"What on earth have you brought home this time?" she called, amused.

Tom stopped the truck in front of his wife, turned off the engine, and got out. He was enormously glad that his wife had a good sense of humor and knew what a pushover he was when it came to his children.

"Well, apparently, two horses aren't enough. We have now increased our herd by one and a half," Tom quipped. "Apparently, we're also shy on blonds so we brought home another one."

"Oh? And exactly what is wrong with blonds?" Mary chuckled, the laugh lines around her eyes crinkling.

"Not a thing," Tom cried as he tugged down the ramp. "I'm quite partial to blonds myself. I'm even partial to building my wife a new garden shed."

"And a good thing too," his wife nodded. "I expect you'll be picking up the lumber tomorrow."

"I expect I will," Tom agreed with a wink.

"Wait until you see her, Mom," Linda yelled. "She's so beautiful that it almost makes you wanta cry."

"Is she now?" Mary responded, wiping the flour from her hands on her apron. She stepped down from the porch and watched her husband unload the filly.

Easter walked down the ramp and looked around at her new home, her ears forward and her eyes sparkling with interest. Sal and Pizzazz whinnied from their paddock on the far side of the barn. Easter squealed out a greeting. The old horse blanket had slipped sideways; the filly looked like she had a large green and grey lump of fungus growing out of her stomach. Her face was slick and wet, her white blaze dazzlingly bright.

"Good lord!" Mary exclaimed.

Tom raised an eyebrow. "It's a long story," he said.

"I'm guessing that it's quite an interesting one as well," Mary offered. She chuckled. "She does have a very pretty head and lovely, kind eyes."

"Wait until you see her with the blanket off. She has four white stockings and the shiniest golden coat. She's all dappled, kinda like a bunch of soap bubbles burst on her chest and flanks. Mr. Sims, he was Easter's owner. Oh, yeah. That's her name...Easter, I mean," Linda babbled. "Her mother's name was Ester and Ester died a few days after Mrs. Sims. Easter was born on Easter, that's why she's named that. 'She's a miracle', that's what Mrs.

Worthing says. Mrs. Worthing is Mr. Sims' housekeeper and she makes really good cookies. Dad invited them both for dinner next Sunday."

"Okay," Linda's mother held up her hands. "Get that horse settled in, then give me the long, slow version."

"Come on, Sweet Pea. Your mother is right! You've got a horse to look after," Tom gently chided his daughter. "That was the arrangement, remember?"

Linda grinned and took the lead line from her father's out-stretched hand. Ross straightened out the filly's blanket before Linda led Easter towards the barn.

Tom moved the truck and trailer out of the way, then followed his wife and kids to the stables, the dark look on his face deepening.

Linda released Easter into one of the stalls while Ross went and got the filly some hay and water. Tom went into the tack room and came back carrying a fleecy blue stall blanket which he tossed over the stable door before entering the stall. He removed the worn rug from the filly's back and gave her a good check over.

"She's swollen up in the legs and still feverish. We'll have Doc Martin come and check her out tonight if she's still hot in an hour or so. I expect it's just stress from the auction and the travellin'," Tom said. He slipped the winter fleece blanket over her head and tugged it down over her back, then rubbed the palomino on the poll. The filly grunted and pushed into his hand. Tom smiled. "She sure is a nice filly, Sweet Pea. You're gonna have to take real good care of this girl. Don't forget to phone Mr. Sims later to let him know she's okay."

"You bet I will," Linda chimed. "I'll call him right after Easter is settled in." Easter nibbled at Linda's pockets, looking for treats.

"You want me to bring the girls in, Dad?" asked Ross.

Tom nodded, his wife standing wordlessly beside him.

Mary had already judged her husband's temper and decided not to ask any more questions. It was clear by his stiff shoulders and the smirk on his face that there was more to the story of Easter than she had already been told.

Ross went out and brought Sal and Pizzazz into the barn. Both mares stopped and tried to sniff the newcomer. Ross kept them away for now, not wanting the filly to get more upset. The mares seemed happy enough to be brought in out of the rain and settled down quickly in the stalls across the aisle from Easter. The air in the barn quickly warmed up with all three horses inside.

The filly visibly relaxed. Sal squealed and thumped a leg against a stall door.

"Now, Sally, I'll be over to give you a brush in a minute," Linda scolded the Fjord.

Sal snorted and pinned back her ears; her temper strained by the lack of attention Linda was showing her.

"Don't you be forgettin' old Sally just because Easter is here," her father said.

"I won't," Linda promised. "Cross my heart."

Tom turned and closed the stall door behind him. "You give all three mares a brushin', then come in for dinner. If Easter is still lathered up after dinner, I'll call the vet."

48

"You think she needs Doc Martin already?" Mary blurted out.

"She's younger than she looks," was all her husband would say.

Mary pursed her lips together. She understood the problem now. A pregnant horse meant vet bills. It was clear that her daughter adored the palomino; she had been hinting that she wanted a new horse for some time. Tom had given in to his daughter's wishes and was probably regretting it.

Linda nodded and her father smiled at her.

Tom abruptly turned on his heels and bent down to kiss his wife on the cheek. Mary giggled. He gazed into his wife's eyes and shrugged helplessly. Mary dipped an arm under his and kissed him back.

"Don't be too long," he said to his daughter.

"I won't," promised Linda.

Ross winked at his little sister and followed his parents up to the house.

"It's okay, Sally," Linda said over the stall door, "I'll be there in a minute. I just know that you and Easter are gonna be real good friends. It's just that Easter isn't feelin' well at the moment on account of her bein' in foal."

Sally snorted and stuck her head into her hay bin. She pulled out a leaf of hay and shook it from side to side like a dog with a rope. Pizzazz watched quietly as Linda fussed over the filly, not caring one way or the other so long as there was food in front of her. The tall, grey mare was Ross' horse. Pizzazz was picky about who she let touch her. When Ross wasn't around, she preferred to be left alone.

Linda finished cuddling her new horse and went to get her brushes. She groomed the mud off Sal first... a big job since Sally had hair as thick and plush as a down-filled pillow and loved to wallow in the mud until there wasn't a patch of hair on her body left clean. Linda coughed as she brushed Sal, the mud flaking away in a thick cloud of dust; it clogged her nostrils and stung her lungs. She went to work on Pizzazz, a chore which didn't take long as Pizzazz was the opposite of Sal. She hated getting dirty. Before Linda knew it, her mother was calling her into the house for dinner.

Linda gave the three horses a pat, switched off the lights and headed up to the farmhouse. With a start, she realized that she hadn't called Mr. Sims to let him know that they had arrived safely. She bolted across the yard, splashing through puddles, and pushed open the kitchen door. The door banged shut behind her. Waffles woofed at her from under the kitchen table. She saw Mr. Sims' number scribbled on a piece of paper taped to the wall beside the phone and eagerly tapped out his number.

Linda shoveled down her dinner, much to the disapproval of her mother. Her mother insisted that the whole family wait until the coffee was ready and the table cleared before going to the barn to check on the filly. Linda hopped from foot to foot as she stood at the sink washing the last of the dinner dishes, Ross drying them and putting them away at her side.

Coffee cups in hand, her parents walked casually across the yard behind their daughter and son. The wind had died down and the rain had stopped. The night was dark and misty. The overhead light above the stable entrance dripped with water, a puddle forming at the base of the door under which it hung. Waffles snuffled around the door, his tail wagging constantly.

Waffles provided constant amusement for the McClouds. He had been given to them when their old dog had passed away and the old woman who owned him realized he needed more space that her apartment's small patio could offer. Waffles was called Waffles because Waffles loved waffles and he'd scratch a hole in the kitchen door if he was outside and smelled maple syrup. Tom had installed a dog door two days after they got him. From there, it was only one flight of stairs to Linda's bedroom, and then to her bed. The McClouds joked that he was the only farm dog in the district that ruled the house as well as the barn.

Linda pulled open the stable door and flipped the light switch, just inside the entry. The air was warm and musty; it smelled of sawdust, hay and horses. The lights overhead glowed dully. The three mares nickered a greeting and hung their heads over their stall doors.

The horses were quite a motley crew. Sal's large cream colored head, topped with a black and white striped mane and forelock, bobbed up and down, her short Mohawk haircut bristling. Pizzazz' pink nostrils flared, her grey face and white blaze, dainty and pretty. Pizzazz was sharp and intelligent; she never missed a thing. Easter was relaxed, tucked cozily inside her stall. She seemed happy to have company.

"Hi, girls!" Tom called out.

"Hey, Sally. Hey, Easter," Linda said, roaming from Sally to Easter.

Ross went straight to Pizzazz. He gave her a pat and a small chunk of apple that he had smuggled out of the house. Sal stretched her head towards him, wondering where her piece was. When Ross ignored her, she sunk her teeth into his jeans and tore off his back pocket.

"Sally!" Ross growled.

"That'll teach you," his mother replied, fixing Ross with 'the look' that meant that it served him right. 'Give a treat to one, give a treat to all' was her motto.

Tom handed his coffee cup to his wife and went in the stall with Easter. He pulled off the blanket. Easter's chest, shoulders and flanks were dark with sweat. A light layer of foam gathered under her forelegs and inside her hind legs.

"My, she is gorgeous...and she certainly is very pregnant," Mary said.

"Yeah and she's only two," Ross added, walking over to stand beside his mother.

"Good lord. You didn't tell me that she was that young!" Mary exclaimed.

"I don't much like her sweatin' like this. Ross, go and call Doc Martin. Let's have him take a look at her anyway," Tom said, the lines on his forehead deepening. "Linda, go and get a towel and let's give her a rub down."

Linda ran to the tack room. Ross went up to the house and phoned the vet. Linda came back with a couple of towels and watched her father gently rub down the filly.

"Her breathin' is a bit heavy," Tom commented.

"When is she due?" his wife asked.

"Not for another six weeks," he said dryly.

52

"She's due on Easter?" Mary asked, shocked.

"Weird, isn't it, Mom? She was born on Easter and her foal is due on Easter," Linda added. She leaned against the stall door, worried for her filly, but knowing that Doc Martin was one of the best vets around.

"That is strange," Mary replied, then took a sip of coffee.

Ross came back into the barn. "Doc Martin is down at the Joes. One of their cows is down. He said that he's almost done and he'll be here shortly."

"That's good," Tom nodded, happy that they weren't going to have to wait for several hours. He'd feel a lot better once Doc Martin looked at the filly.

It wasn't long before Doc Martin's Chevy pulled into the yard. He walked into the barn, a short broad-shouldered man with salty hair and a purposeful stride. Doc Martin didn't waste time or words, both were too precious. He had a large black duffel bag in one hand and was dressed in green coveralls.

"So, Linda. I hear that you're expecting?" Doc Martin said amiably.

"Yep. Her name's Easter and I'm hopin' that she'll give me another pretty palomino filly just like her." Linda grinned, liking the vet.

"Well, let's take a good look at her," Doc Martin finished, opening the door to the stall.

Tom stepped back and let Doc Martin examine the filly.

The vet opened his bag and pulled out a stethoscope. He listened to the filly's heart, then proceeded to move it down her belly. He worked quickly and quietly. Easter sighed and accepted his ministrations without biting or kicking.

Doc Martin gave her a full checkup and stepped back.

"She's a lovely girl, your Easter. Her heart is strong and so is the foal's. I'm a little concerned about her age as well. Her breathing is a bit off, but not enough to worry about yet. She is running a slight temperature. I'm going to give you some mild antibiotics to fight whatever it is that she's picked up at the auction yard...not a big surprise that is. Still can't believe where you found her," the Doc said, shaking his head in disbelief. "She's a gem, this one. Don't you worry, we'll keep a close eye on her. I'll pop by tomorrow to see how she's doing."

"Thanks, Doc," Tom replied.

"Meantime, keep her warm and dry," Doc Martin advised. "Keep her away from the other two mares until this fever clears up too! I don't want her passing around whatever she's got. Hopefully it's just the stress and the pregnancy."

"Okay," Tom agreed.

"It's strange for a filly this young to catch like that," the vet said.

"We were just talking about that," Mary added.

"Can you tell if she's havin' a colt or a filly?" Linda asked sweetly.

Ross and his father choked back a laugh.

"Seems, Doc, that my kids are split. Linda wants a filly and Ross wants a colt," Tom offered in explanation.

"Do you really want to know?" Doc Martin offered.

"No," Mary said crossly. "It should be a surprise, just like the two of you were," she commanded.

Tom and the kids giggled.

"Mother has spoken," Doc Martin returned. He chuckled and packed up his bag. "I'm looking forward to seeing what she throws myself. If she throws a palomino colt and you want to sell him, I want first shot at buying him."

"You'll have to fight me off first," Ross said.

"It's not gonna be a colt; it's gonna be a filly," Linda argued stubbornly.

With that, Doc Martin gave Easter a shot of antibiotics and took off to his next call.

"Can I sleep out here with Easter?" Linda asked after the doctor had left.

"No!" Tom and Mary said together.

Linda was crestfallen.

"I'll stay with you until it's time to get ready for bed," Ross consoled her. "I've got chores to finish anyway."

"Okay. I'll help you," Linda sniffled.

Tom and Mary went back into the house, leaving Linda and Ross to feed and water the cattle in the second barn out back. Linda ran back to check on Easter so often that Ross told her to stay with the filly until it was time to go in.

With a sad face, Linda turned off the lights and bid the horses a good night. She prayed that Easter would be feeling better in the morning.

# Chapter Five

## Out Like a Lion

Linda watched her mother, father, and brother leave for Cold River. For four weeks, they had all fretted over Easter until finally her mother insisted that they get off the farm for awhile. Ross was delighted to be able to visit Jenny on the way into town; he hadn't seen her for two weeks. Easter's pregnancy was getting more and more difficult so someone had to stay and look after her at all times. Since it was Linda's horse, she was elected. Her father left all the vet's phone numbers scribbled down on pieces of paper beside the phone in the kitchen and tacked to Easter's stall door inside the barn with instructions to check on the pregnant cows regularly as well. Her mother had cheerily given her a peck on the cheek on the way out the door and a list of chores to do.

Linda wasn't sure how her mother expected her to keep an eye on Easter and the cows while vacuuming the big four bedroom farmhouse, washing the breakfast dishes, dusting the living room and cleaning up her room. It didn't make any sense to Linda so she decided to throw on her jacket and muck boots and go clean the barn instead.

Linda closed the kitchen door behind her and stood for a moment on the porch. Overhead a strong breeze chased the clouds around in the sky like a Border Collie herding sheep. To the northwest, the horizon was dark and forbidding, the cloud cover thick and sinister. It pushed aside the candyfloss clouds and shut out the sun, rolling across the fields like a plague of locusts. The beautiful, warm sunny morning disappeared quickly as the storm that had gathered over the far away mountains overnight began to blow in.

"I don't like the look of that," Linda muttered, staring at the building storm clouds. Waffles let out a low woof from inside his dog house. He only used the house when he felt like it or when he was scared. "You don't either, do you?" she said, turning to the dog.

Waffles stood up and strolled out of his house, stopped to stretch and yawn, then walked across the porch to Linda. His winter coat was shedding out; his black and tan fur was dull and uneven. He sat down beside her and leaned against her leg. Linda reached down and rubbed the dog's large head. Thick clumps of downy fur came off in her hands. She sneezed and rubbed her hands on her jeans, trying to scrape off the hair that clung to her fingers and coat sleeves.

A strong gust of wind rattled the wind chimes fastened to the rafters at the end of the porch and rippled across the puddles in the yard. The shepherd cowed and whined softly. Linda idly scratched him behind the ears. The dog's tail thumped loudly on the wooden porch.

"I hope Mom and Dad aren't too late getting back," Linda said to Waffles. He looked up at her; his eyes were large and trusting.

Linda checked her coat pockets, pulled out her brother's cell phone and pushed the little red button to turn it on. She breathed a small sigh of relief and tucked the phone safely back in her pocket.

She stepped off the porch and saw their neighbor, Ole Man Levy, leave his house and get into his rusty Dodge pick-up truck. The old man wore the same dirty, battered John Deere cap pulled down over his hawkish face and faded red-checkered shirt that he always did. Linda was glad that she didn't have to listen to him shout at the old white pony anymore. She shivered inside her jacket; Ole Man Levy gave her the creeps!

The old man looked at her through the truck's window. He never waved or nodded, just ignored her and skidded out of the driveway in a hail of gravel, turning left, heading for River Bend. He ate most of his meals at Mom's Restaurant and Bakery. Linda guessed that was where he was going. She didn't know whether to be glad that he was leaving or worried that she was all alone with no one around for at least a mile in each direction.

"What do you think, Waffles? Think I should call Johnny or Hannah and ask one of them to come up and stay with us?"

Waffles whined and barked.

"You're right. Johnny will have chores to do, but I bet Hannah would ride Frosty over."

The dog barked twice, his tail thumping harder on the porch at the mention of Hannah's name. Linda laughed and kissed the dog on top of his head. He cried and licked her cheek.

Linda sauntered across the muddy yard, her boots squelching, heading for the stable. The front section of the two-storey red barn housed the three horses, the back of it was an open loafing shed that the cattle could walk in and out of as they pleased during the winter, and the upper level was filled with row on row of hay. The McCloud farm was close to 500 acres; it had originally been over four times that size, but over the years, the family had sold most of it. They had 300 acres in high quality timothy and alfalfa hay, most of which they sold off, 100 in corn, 50 in pasture, and the rest in marshy woodlands. A tall, silver grain silo and rusty grain elevator stood sentinel behind the barn.

Linda pulled the cell phone out of her pocket and dialed Hannah's number. It rang twice before Hannah picked up the phone.

"Hi, Hannah?" Linda asked. She stopped outside the barn door knowing that sometimes the cell didn't work inside the stable.

"Hey, Linda. What's up? Is Easter okay?" Hannah asked, her voice going from cheery to worried.

"She's fine. Can you ride up and stay with me for awhile? Mom and Dad took Ross to see Jenny and are doin' a big shoppin' run in Cold River. I kinda don't like being alone out here with Easter havin' such a hard time. I've got four cows to watch over too."

"Sure. I can ride Frosty over. Do you want me to bring Johnny? I don't know how much help that I'll be. I don't know anything about pregnant horses or cows," Hannah said seriously.

"No, that's okay. If Easter starts sweatin' up again, then I can call the vet and you can maybe go and get Johnny and his dad for me," Linda said thoughtfully. "I know that Johnny probably still has lots of chores to do. I sure do!"

Hannah laughed.

"I'll see you in about half an hour."

Linda grinned. "Thanks, Hannah."

"See you!"

Linda flipped the top of the cell phone closed and smiled. Waffles barked.

"That was easy. Maybe Hannah will offer to help with my chores," she said to the dog as she pulled open the barn door.

Easter whinnied a greeting from inside her box stall. Pizzazz and Sal squealed and thumped their legs against their stall doors. None of the horses were happy about being inside. The barn's rafters creaked and groaned above them. The wind blowing through the cracks in the walls ruffled their manes.

"Well, I guess I can let you girls out for an hour while I clean your stalls," Linda piped.

She wandered by Easter and gave the filly a quick pat.

"I'm just gonna put Sal and Pizzazz out first, Easter, then I'll be back for you."

The filly snorted and playfully nipped Linda's jacket. Linda glanced over the stall door and was pleased to see that the palomino wasn't sweaty like she had been the last four weeks. The filly's breathing was regular and there didn't appear to be any swelling in her legs either.

Doc Martin popped by every chance he got to check on her.

"You look good today, girl! I'll let you out for a little fresh air too, but don't do anything silly like runnin' around and buckin' or anything because I'll have to bring you back in," she scolded the mare gently. Easter licked her lips and nodded. Linda laughed heartily.

Pizzazz wheeled in her stall and screamed louder.

"Alright! Keep your knickers on, Zazzy. I'm comin'," Linda muttered as she picked up a halter and opened Pizzazz' stall door. Pizzazz tried to bolt by her, but Linda lifted a hand and scooted her back into the stall. She reached out and gently rubbed the grey mare's muzzle, then stepped forward and slipped the halter on over her head. Pizzazz danced on the spot, eager to be outside romping in what was left of the sunshine.

Linda led the tall grey mare out of the barn and unhooked the lead rope. Pizzazz let out a giant buck and bolted, tail in the air, across the field to join the herd of Limousin cattle that grazed on the winter grasses at the back of the farm. Sal whinnied sadly from inside her stall. The two mares had been together for eight years.

Linda returned and put a halter on Sal. The Fjord tucked her head down obediently and let Linda do what she wanted. Linda fussed over her and gave her a good rub down. The old mare sighed with pleasure. Linda stood back and inspected the little blond Fjord. She grunted, satisfied with her efforts. She let Sal go outside and watched her gallop off to join Pizzazz. The mare's fat belly jiggled from side to side as she thundered down the path to the back pasture, her hooves leaving deep ruts in the soggy earth, her Mohawk bobbing from side to side as she ran.

"Hmmm. Sally needs a haircut, Waffles," she murmured to the dog at her heels.

Linda ambled down the path that the horses had just run down and stopped at the first fence line. She undid the clip that held the gate open and closed the gate, blocking off the bottom pasture from the barnyard. She didn't want Easter to go galloping off to join the others; it wasn't safe for her. She heard Easter nicker, calling out for company.

"I'm comin," Linda yelled to the filly, almost losing a boot in the foot deep mud as she climbed back up the hill to the stable. "You're learnin' bad habits from Pizzazz!"

Waffles bolted by her and around the barn. Linda figured that he must have scented a rabbit; either that, or Ole Man Levy had returned back home. Waffles didn't like Ole Man Levy any better than she did.

"Maybe Waffles hears Frosty and Hannah comin'," Linda said to Easter as she kicked the mud off her boots against the stall door. She'd sweep it up later, after it dried. She rubbed the soft downy spot on the filly's nose, then slipped a halter over her head and fastened it up. Linda slid a hand under the filly's fleecy stall blanket and felt her breathing. It was steady and even. She checked the blanket's belly band, making sure the back straps were fine, then pushed open the stall door. Easter waited patiently for Linda to lead her outside.

With a snort of pleasure, she whinnied at Pizzazz and Sal down in the fields. The two mares looked up and whinnied back, then put their heads back down to eat. The wind rushed across the pastures, ruffling the bushes along the ditch that bordered the highway to the north. Easter squealed and let out a small buck.

"Enough of that now," Linda chided the filly and unclasped the lead line.

The filly grunted and wandered away from Linda, her great fat belly bulging out on either side of the blanket. She tucked her legs beneath her and laid down on the ground, letting out a huge sigh of happiness. She rubbed her belly back and forth in the mud, rested and did it again.

"What's she doing?" a voice called from over to the left.

"Oh!" Linda jumped, startled. "I didn't know the time had gone that fast. I haven't even done the stalls yet."

Hannah burst out laughing. A white head appeared beside Hannah's and leaned over the fence. Frosty nickered shrilly at the filly. Easter looked up, but continued to rock back and forth on the ground, her front legs splayed out straight in front of her, her rear legs tucked up tight underneath.

"She's placing the foal," Linda said, turning towards Hannah.

"She's what?" Hannah asked, her black hair falling forward over her face, hiding her sparkling blue eyes.

"See how she's rolling on one side, then onto the other? She's positioning the foal so that she'll feel more comfortable and to make sure it'll be born the right way up," Linda responded.

Hannah's gelding, Frosty, watched the filly with interest. His frostbitten ears were pricked forward, the white hairs on his neck quivering. He arched his head over the fence, his black eyes fixed on the golden palomino with the bright white blaze down her forehead.

"Cosmo!" Hannah quipped.

"Coolio!" Linda answered back.

The girls giggled.

"Doc Martin says that she's only got about a week or two now. She's been much better this last month and she sure has got attached to Sal and Pizzazz," Linda volunteered. "I hope she ends up foaling on Easter."

"That'd be really coolio!" Hannah said. "What'll you call the foal though? You already have an Easter."

"I'm not sure yet," Linda said, one eyebrow raised. "Ross and Dad told me that it's bad luck to name the foal before it's born. Doc Martin said he could tell me if it was a colt or a filly, but I want it to be a surprise. That way, when she has a filly, I can give my brother a hard time forever!"

"Better listen then," Hannah nodded in agreement. She grinned. "Ross will certainly be miffed if she doesn't throw a colt! That's all he talks about at school. He's worse than you."

"Yeah, even Jenny's complaining about it," Linda replied. "This is like finding a Christmas present hidden away that you know is for you, but you just can't figure out what it is no matter how hard you try!"

A great gust of wind shook the barn to its foundation. A few scattered snowflakes fell from the sky. The clouds grew darker and more ominous.

"I can't believe this! March 26th and it's starting to snow again," Hannah whined and looked up. "I want to move back to Vancouver where it's warm."

"No you don't, you couldn't stand the city anymore. In like a lamb and out like a lion! You wait, this will be the last one, I'm sure of it. Spring is just around the corner. Right now, you better put Frosty in Sal's stall and I'll get Easter up," Linda added, moving fast. The filly was still laying on the ground, not bothering to try to stand up, despite the icy snowflakes that blanketed her back and painted her whole face white.

Waffles barked. The girls heard a shout and the sound of hoof beats. Hannah looked over her shoulder. Frosty nickered.

"It's Johnny and Charlie Horse! He must have seen me riding up here," Hannah exclaimed.

The snow fell harder. Thick white flakes jigged and swirled around in little eddies on the ground as the wind picked up speed. Within a couple of minutes, Linda could barely see the horses and the cattle in the bottom pasture.

"I think I'm gonna need some help with the cattle," Linda said.

"Go right into the barn," Hannah called to Johnny, her arm waving him on as she disappeared with Frosty around the side of the stable.

Linda heard the barn doors slide open and ran to Easter's side.

The filly stretched her nose up to Linda, her pink nostrils flaring. Linda brushed the snow from her face and stroked the white hairs of Easter's blaze. She clipped the lead line to the halter ring and lifted the filly's head up gently. Easter grunted, pushed her great bulk forwards, but couldn't get her back legs well enough underneath her belly to lift herself to her feet. She bent one

65

front leg underneath her massive bulk and heaved upwards, but wasn't strong enough to bear her own weight.

"Come on, Easter, you've gotta get up," Linda cried.

The palomino grunted and groaned, tried once more to get to her feet, but stumbled and landed heavily to one side. Easter's eyes grew wild and glassy. Sweat broke out on her neck and her breathing grew ragged as she struggled for breath.

"You guys! I need help!" Linda shouted.

Johnny and Hannah quickly emerged through the barn's back door. They slid across the muddy yard, coming to an abrupt stop beside Linda. Johnny's dark eyes immediately took in the situation. His black hair was freckled with a white powdering of snow and his brows were furrowed in concentration.

"Hannah, go call the vet!" he ordered.

Linda yanked the cell phone out of her pocket and threw it to Hannah. Hannah snatched the phone out of the air with shaking hands.

"The vet's numbers are on Easter's stall. Try his cell phone first," Linda said, her voice trembling.

Hannah flipped the phone open as she ran inside the barn.

"I want you to stay at her head and keep her calm," Johnny said. "I'm gonna go to the back of her and grab hold of her tail. Hannah can help you when she gets back. I want both you girls to pull her forward and I'm gonna pull her up from the back, try to steady her that way. Okay?"

Linda nodded, tears forming at the corner of her eyes. She wished that she had never let Easter out of her stall.

"Don't worry, Easter," she crooned, half-heartedly. "You're gonna be fine."

Johnny walked around the back of the filly as she lay patiently on the ground, her sides heaving, her breath a frosty stream in front of her face. He cooed to her as if she was a baby and untangled her long silken tail from between her hind legs. He tied the end of it in a knot and grabbed a good hold. The filly's mane, whiskers and blanket were covered in a thin layer of white snow.

"The vet's on the way," Hannah gasped breathlessly as she skittered to a stop beside Linda, her arms wind-milling sideways to keep from falling on top of the filly.

"Hannah, grab one side of the halter and a fist full of mane. Linda, you just pull from the other side," Johnny commanded.

Hannah did as she was told. Easter shied away from her at first, but Linda calmed her down with a soothing pat. Hannah stroked the filly's neck with one hand and ran the fingers of the other through Easter's silken mane, then closed her fingers into a fist and held on tight.

"Okay, Easter. Up!" Linda urged the filly on by lifting up on the headstall.

Easter moaned in protest and struggled to get to her feet, her hind legs slipping on the mud. Johnny pulled her tail in the direction that the filly was trying to heave herself upright.

"Come on, Easter, you can do it!" Linda yelled, tugging forwards on Easter's halter for all she was worth.

Hannah strained and pushed against the filly's neck, her cheeks reddening with the effort. Sweat broke out on her upper lip. She clenched her jaw. Her blue eyes danced with a cold fire as she tried to lift Easter to her feet through sheer will power alone.

The little filly screamed and lurched upwards, her front legs splaying, her pregnant belly rolling back and forth. Johnny pushed her from behind, then scooted out of the way as the horse got her back hooves firmly underneath her and regained her balance.

"Yeah!" Linda cheered.

The filly snorted and groaned, her body weaving from side to side, still somewhat unsteady.

"Get her into her stall quickly," Johnny ordered.

"Come on, Easter, you silly little girl," Linda said sweetly, leading the filly back into the stable. Easter stopped and stretched her hind legs, then walked slowly into her stall after her master.

The snowstorm gathered speed; ice pellets pelted against the barn's siding. It took all three kids to roll the barn door shut. The snow covered the ground in a clean layer of white silk, hiding the mud and filling in the puddles.

"What about Sal and Pizzazz?" Hannah asked, peeking out at the storm through a crack in the door, her mouth open in disbelief at how fast the storm had descended. It seemed like only moments ago that she was trotting Frosty down the highway and enjoying the bright sunshine.

"Oh, no! The girls! The gate is shut! We need to open the far gate so that the cows can get into the loafing barn too!" Linda squealed, her eyes filling with tears.

"Where is it?" Johnny asked.

"Go down to the bottom of the paddock and turn right. I already closed that gate so that Easter couldn't run away. There is another gate on the far side of that which needs to be opened to let the cattle in. I was gonna fire up the tractor and clean out both sides of the barn so Ross shut that one for me this morning," Linda cried.

"Don't worry. I've bin out in worse." Johnny chuckled and tugged on his gloves. He pulled the zipper up on his jacket and slipped open the barn door. The wind howled through the stable, the snow whirl-pooling along the floor. The girls pushed it shut behind him.

Horses whinnied shrilly in the distance, their high-pitched calls rising above the sound of cattle mooing from within a swirling cloud of white. Charlie Horse, Johnny's large bay Quarter Horse nickered, Frosty adding his comments on the matter too as Johnny disappeared into the snowstorm.

"I better call my mom and let her know that we're okay," Hannah said, her eyes fixed on the door through which Johnny had disappeared. Her hands shook as she tried to tap out her home number on the cell phone's pad.

"I think Easter is gonna be fine," Linda replied, walking over and placing a hand on the filly's chest. "She's stopped heavin' so hard and I can see the baby kicking."

The filly's side rippled and moved, the foal kicking up its own storm inside its momma's belly. The filly snorted and nuzzled Linda's arm. Linda chuckled.

"That must hurt!" Linda lifted a hand, brushing the snow from her horse's forelock. She turned to Hannah and pointed to the far side of the stable. "Hannah, there's a bale of hay by the tack room, over there. I think you and

69

Johnny are gonna be here awhile so we may as well feed everybody."

"Yeah," Hannah said absently, closing the top on the cell phone. "The phone's not connecting. It must be the storm. I guess our lines are out." She walked over to where Linda had pointed and came back with an armful of hay. The horses whinnied softly and kicked at the stall doors. "I hope Johnny doesn't get lost out there."

"He won't! All he has to do is follow the fence line in," Linda said wisely.

Just then, they heard a bang and the ground shook under their feet. The sounds of cattle bawling filled the air.

"That would be him now," Linda giggled.

Hannah let out a weary sigh of relief.

Johnny burst into the stable through the small door in the wall that separated the stable from the main barn. Waffles scooted out from between his legs, his tongue lolling to one side, his eyes feverishly bright. Both Johnny and the dog were covered with snow. They shook themselves off in the alley between the stalls.

"How's Easter?" he asked, making his way towards the girls. His horse reached his head over the stall door. Johnny gave him a quick pat as he walked by. "It's really bad out there; there is no way the vet is gonna make it."

"I think she's okay," Linda responded, grateful that Johnny was there. Johnny always seemed older than his thirteen years.

Johnny pulled back the blanket and checked the mare's breathing and felt her belly. He grinned, his eyes sparkling. "Cheeky little foal, you've got, Miss Easter."

He tugged the blanket back into place and reached underneath to check her milk bags.

"I swear that foal just tried to nip me right through Easter's tummy." He grinned. "Yeah, she's alright. Feels like her temperature is down and she's not wobbly anymore. She's not drippin' any milk either so her milk sack hasn't bagged up yet."

"Thank goodness," Linda croaked. If Easter was spouting milk, that would mean that the foal was on the way. With all of Easter's problems, Linda knew that the three of them couldn't handle it alone!

"You stay with your filly and Hannah and I will go drop down some feed for the cattle. Sal and Pizzazz are happy in the loafing barn with the cattle. Sal blends right in; it's hard to tell her apart from the cows. I don't think I've ever seen a horse that dirty before."

"Thank you so much, Johnny," Linda threw her arms around the older boy's neck. "I don't know what I'd have done without you."

"Watch out. I don't want Hannah gettin' jealous," he said playfully.

Hannah swatted his arm. "Just for that," she said, "I'll un-tack our horses and you go feed everyone else."

"Whoops," Johnny rolled his eyes at Linda, knowing that he deserved that.

The cell phone rang shrilly in Hannah's pocket.

"I bet that's my mom," Linda quipped.

"Tell them not to rush," Johnny said. "We're all okay. Call the vet back too. It won't hurt for him to check on Easter, but I don't think it needs to be an emergency call now. That filly's pretty strong and this storm's bound to

71

blow over fairly quickly," Johnny said. "I bet that it'll be pouring rain in a half hour!"

Linda agreed as Hannah gave her back the phone. Linda thought the wind sounded less ominous than it had only moments ago, but maybe that was her imagination.

# Chapter Six

## *Mom's Restaurant & Bakery*

The old man saw young Linda McCloud staring at him from across the highway. Her full moon face and long blond hair reminded him so much of his daughter, Eliza, that it took his breath away and sent cold shivers up and down his spine. He and Eliza hadn't spoken a word to each other in ten years; not since his granddaughter, Kathy, had taken a fall off the little white mustang and broken her leg and collar bone.

He had thought he'd done the right thing, buying the white mustang from the Cree Reservation up north. He wanted to mend the fences that his wife, Sarah, said he'd not just erected, but built as high as the Heavens themselves. Kathy had been thrilled and really loved the pony.

It was funny, he thought, how he couldn't even remember what Kathy had named the mustang. He guessed it was the living alone that did it: no one to talk to, no one to discuss the day with and no one to remind you of what went on in the past. He'd taken his hatred of

73

life out on the pony and was ashamed of it now, but he realized after he bought the mustang that it was a mistake. That pony had a meanness in him that went right to the bone...he had a dark, crazy look that crept into his eyes like Satan himself was inside the mustang's skin and looking right at him. He knew it was a crazy thought, but he just couldn't stop it.

Eliza hadn't wanted Kathy to learn to ride. Eliza hated horses. Eliza hated cattle. Eliza hated everything that reminded her of life on the farm. She had run off to the city at seventeen and never looked back. It wasn't until she married Gerry and had Kathy that she bothered to phone and tell her mother about it.

Gerry was a good husband and father. He figured it was Gerry that made her call her mother. She hadn't talked to him when she phoned, only to Sarah.

The old man spat a wad of brown chewing tobacco onto the ground and climbed into his rusty Dodge. The girl across the road continued to stare at him, her mouth slightly open, her posture rigid. If he yelled "Boo!" out the window, he thought she might drop dead on the ground. It was the same look that Eliza used to give him the whole time she was growing up.

The old man pressed his foot down on the accelerator and sped out of the driveway in a torrent of flying gravel. He couldn't stand to see the look on the girl's face anymore. It made him feel empty and more than a little sick to his stomach. Course, he reasoned, he had gas and that was probably what was making him feel so bad.

He hunkered down inside his jacket as he pulled into town, not liking the company at Mom's Restaurant and

74

Bakery any more than he liked being alone all the time, but it broke the monotony of watching TV.

The bell above the door jangled when he entered the restaurant. Everyone stopped talking at once. He didn't mind; he was used to it. The smell of fresh made bread and perking coffee that greeted him made his mouth water. The delicious scents covered the underlying smell of cow manure and mud. He was surprised that almost every table was full; usually, it was less than a third filled at this time of day. He wondered why?

He nodded to Bill and Kurt Johansen and grunted at Momma Lotham as he sat down at an empty two-seater table. Bill lifted a hand in greeting; they used to be good friends, but the old man had shied away from all friendship after Sarah passed away despite Bill's offers of help. He just didn't feel sociable anymore with Sarah gone.

Momma Lotham bustled over with a full pot of coffee and poured him a steaming black cupful.

"The usual?" she asked.

"Yessum," he answered.

Momma Lotham turned and waddled back to the counter, plunked the coffee pot back down on the warmer, and yelled into the kitchen, "Stew and taters, Sam. Extra dumplings!"

The old man sat back in his chair and took a sip of coffee. It burned his throat on the way down. He listened intently as the conversation resumed all around him. He grinned slightly as his eye fell on the strange painting of Mom's Restaurant that hung proudly on the wall behind the cash register. That crazy Storey woman had painted it. It was the weirdest picture that he'd ever seen: wide brush strokes, thick slashes of bright yellow paint, the bakery windows reflecting a prairie sky as blue and worn as faded denims, the sign for Mom's Restaurant and Bakery a thin scar of sunset red. She'd created quite a ruckus when she set herself up in the middle of the street with her easel and her paints, wild music blaring from the ghetto blaster propped against her feet. She didn't even flinch when a big rig made its way around her. The old man chortled in amusement. Folks in town still whispered about that day as if an alien had landed in the middle of Main Street and the secret was to be protected at all costs.

"I tell ya," some fellow that he didn't know muttered behind him. "I heard that filly's already dropped the foal and it had two heads! Heard it from a fellow whose friends with Doc Martin. He swears it's the truth!"

"Two heads? Don't be thick lad," Bill Johansen growled across the aisle. "I know Doc Martin and he never said no such thing!"

Several people at the surrounding tables snickered.

"I heard it was still born," Kurt Johansen, Bill's younger brother said.

"Aye, I heard that too. Seems more than likely considering the filly's so young," Bill agreed. He picked up his cup and finished the last of his brew.

"Naw," a brawny, red haired trucker said from across the restaurant, "I know from a fellow who picked up a load of hay two days ago that the filly had the foal and it twisted her up good. He said she was paralyzed and Tom McCloud's rigged up a sling in the barn so that the foal can still get milk. He said the McCloud girl is plumb crazy over that palomino and wouldn't let her dad put her down. Funniest thing he ever saw, he told me, was seeing that palomino hanging from the ceiling with ropes all over, her legs stuck out as straight as the chair I'm sitting on cause she can't move them."

The old man almost snorted coffee out his nose when he heard that one. The idea that Tom McCloud, or anyone else, would hang a horse from the rafters was nonsense. Momma Lotham returned with a large bowl of stew topped with puffy white dumplings and a fresh pot of coffee. Ole Man Levy nodded his thanks. In the old man's view, listening to all these crackers talk was just as much fun as watching the Storey woman to see if she was going to get run over or not.

"I've had just about enough of this. You men stop talking about things you don't know nothin' about," Momma Lotham ordered, her red face as stern as an army commander's.

"What about it?" Bill asked Ole Man Levy. "You live right across the highway from the McClouds...have you seen that filly with a foal?"

The old man lifted his head and looked his old friend in the eye. He saw Bill flinch and back away from him. Bill knew he should never have asked that question. Even in his prime, the old man wouldn't have answered it. A neighbour's business is a neighbour's business unless he asks you to make it your own! That was how Ole Man Levy viewed life.

"Is that true?" The trucker stood up and sauntered over to the old man's table. He stood hovering over top of him with an air of importance. The trucker smelled of diesel and sweat. He didn't live thereabouts. He worked for Shell Oil and ran tanker trucks north from Edmonton to Fort McMurray, regularly stopping in River Bend for supper three times a week after he delivered a load east of town.

The old man chuckled under his breath, pushed the last of the chewing tobacco against his front teeth and spat it out. It hit the trucker's boots and dripped onto the floor in a muddy brown pool.

"Good Gawd, man, what'd cha do that for?" the trucker shouted, dancing backwards and flicking drops of dark spittle off his boots.

Momma Lotham scuttled back to the old man's table.

"Cause you deserved it; now, get outa here," she pointed towards the door.

Bill and Kurt burst into a hysterical fit of giggles.

The trucker blushed a deep shade of crimson and bolted for the door.

The old man picked up his fork and plunged it into a dumpling. He dug around for awhile. The restaurant went quiet. Bill and Kurt got up and left without another word to him.

The old man stopped playing with the dumplings and looked thoughtful. Bill was right that the filly was far too young to carry the foal without a lot of problems. He had seen Doc Martin pulling into the McClouds' farm too often to doubt that the filly was having a hard time of it. He suspected Tom McCloud rued the day that he bought her.

Ole Man Levy grunted and lifted a fork full of stew and mashed dumpling to his mouth. He paused for a moment and said a small prayer for the girl that looked like his daughter. He hoped that things would turn out alright for her; he'd seen far too much in his seventy-three years and wouldn't wish that kind of pain on anyone. With that, he took a bite of the delicious beef stew and withdrew from the world.

# Chapter Seven

## The Twister

The weather turned overnight; spring was by-passed. The air was hot and humid; the sun was lazy and hot. Horses and cattle shed their winter coats in clumps of hair so thick that it could be knitted into afghans. Birds chirped happily all day long, the sound almost deafening at times. Winter sage brush was replaced by a carpet of green timothy, alfalfa and oat grasses. Reedy patches of bull rushes burst out of muddy ditches and towered over brackish ponds. People whistled happily, their spirits lifting after a long and brutal winter.

Easter was due to have her foal any day, but had developed even more complications. Everyone was worried about her, including Mr. Sims and Mrs. Worthing. Linda phoned them daily with updates, which set Mrs. Worthing into such a tizzy that Mary and Tom McCloud invited the pair to stay at the farm until after the foal was born.

Jen and Sherry called from Cold River every day as well, eager for news. Jen's Grade One class painted a whole series of brightly colored cards wishing Easter well which Mr. Sims picked up on his way to River Bend. The whole McCloud family was touched by the children's kind words and they even seemed to settle Mrs. Worthing down. The cards hung in a festive line on a string across the kitchen window and pegged to the wall over top of the kitchen door. Mrs. Worthing would stare at them, her thoughts adrift, a smile on her lips, as she kneaded dough at the kitchen table.

Johnny and Hannah rode their horses up after school for brief visits as their chores and schoolwork permitted. They endlessly answered questions at school and whenever they were in town collecting groceries or feed. It seemed as if the whole district was holding its breath, eagerly awaiting news about the filly.

At Mom's Restaurant and Bakery, rumors were still flying!

The one piece of gossip that was true was that Easter had asthma. The foal was too big for her young frame to carry, its weight pressing on her lungs and heart. Doc Martin had given Linda a large plastic inhaler tube that fit completely over the horse's nose. It secured around the top of her head with straps and looked like a gas-mask for horses. Ross joked that the palomino was the only horse in the world that could dive underwater and make seahorses jealous. Linda fastened the mask to Easter's nose each morning and evening before spraying a puff of inhaler into the bottom of the mask to open up her lungs. Easter suffered the embarrassment well.

81

Because of the filly's asthma, the barn was too dusty for her. Doc Martin insisted that she be stabled outside as much as possible. Everyone was grateful for the change in weather, including Easter. The filly seemed to brighten up now that she was able to stand outside in the fresh air and bask in the warmth of the spring sunshine.

At first, Linda worried that Easter would lay down again and not be able to get up, but the filly quickly figured out that if she rocked back and forth on her front legs, the momentum would push her forward enough that she could get her hind legs underneath her and she could heave herself upright after a few tries. Mostly, Easter leaned against the side of the barn and gently pushed the foal into position so that it would be born front feet first.

Mrs. Worthing and Mary McCloud kept the kitchen stove fired up. Between the two of them, there was an endless supply of cookies, cakes, and cinnamon buns for anyone that came over. The women had become fast friends in a very short time. Tom teased his wife that they were going to have to build another house on the property to house Will Sims and his housekeeper. Mary thought that a very good idea.

The past two days had been insufferably hot and humid; truly unusual for the first week of April, but prairie weather was unpredictable at the best of times. A thick layer of black low-slung clouds had rolled in and thunder echoed ominously deep within their folds.

"I don't much like the look of that," Tom said to Will Sims as the two men stood side-by-side on the front porch.

"If I didn't know better, I'd say we should move the cattle indoors as we might be seeing a twister before too long," the old man countered, his shoulders still slumped inside his button-downed starched shirt, but his face and eyes much brighter since leaving the lonely house on Knob Hill.

After two days at the McClouds' farm surrounded by people and activity, Will Sims had come back to life. He smiled more often as if a great weight had been lifted from his shoulders.

"Never heard of a twister at this time of year," Tom eyed the heavens, his face etched with worry lines. That was the last thing that anyone in River Bend needed.

Thunder rolled across the river valley. The farmhouse's windows shook. The cattle milled about anxiously in the lower pasture. Merry Penny, the lead cow, mooed loudly and started to amble up the hill towards the barn. The other cattle bawled in answer and tucked themselves in behind her in one long line. The herd would follow her off a cliff if Merry Penny so chose. Pizzazz looked up and snorted, her body quivering at every rumble. Sal ignored everything and kept on eating. Easter whinnied shrilly to the other two mares and moved closer to the stable door, positioning herself under the roof overhang for protection. The animals sensed that there was trouble brewing.

Ross strolled out of the house and onto the porch munching on a peanut butter cookie, Waffles glued to his side and watching every bite he took. He stopped beside his father and looked at the dark sky.

"Should I open up the barn, Dad, and bring all the girls in?" he asked his father.

"No, not yet," his father replied. "If it doesn't blow over in a little while, we will. Merry Penny's bringing the herd up anyway so they'll be close. Easter's better outside until the rain starts. It's painful listening to her breathing so hard when she's in the barn. I can just imagine what it must feel like to her."

Ross nodded and went back into the house, Waffles in hot pursuit.

Johnny and Hannah trotted down the highway, their horses ears pricked forward and their steps high. The air was so unnaturally still that it made the geldings panicky; sweat darkened their necks and fear flared their nostrils. The horses broke into a canter, anxious to get to the McClouds' farm before the storm broke.

Tom and Will saw the kids coming and walked down into the yard. Linda burst out of the barn with a pitchfork in her hand just as her two friends reined their horses up in front of her father. Frosty danced sideways with every peal of thunder, his eyes wild and scared. Charlie Horse snorted and bristled, uncommon for him as he was usually a very placid horse.

"You two took a chance," Tom chastised the pair.

"It was nice when we started out," Hannah said timidly.

"We thought we'd pop in quick and see how Easter was doin', but that storm is rollin' in fast," Johnny said, waiting for Hannah to move Frosty over so he could swing out of the saddle. Once on the ground, he grabbed a hold of Frosty's reins so that Hannah could dismount safely. The little gelding pranced on the spot, the sweat on his neck turning to lather.

"Hi, guys," Linda squealed, leaning the pitchfork against the barn and running towards them.

"Hey," Johnny and Hannah said in unison.

"How's Easter doing?" Hannah asked.

"Her milk bags have dropped. She's gonna foal any time now," Linda said, repeating what the vet had told them earlier that morning.

"You kids get your horses in the barn and come into the house and call your folks," Tom ordered.

"Yes, sir," Johnny nodded.

The three kids walked to the stables. Linda retrieved the pitch fork and helped Johnny and Hannah get the geldings settled.

"This is crazy," Johnny muttered as they ran across the yard towards the house.

"It's scary," Hannah cried out.

Linda nodded in agreement.

The wind started to pick up and whirl bits of dust, gravel and hay around the barnyard. The clouds rotated counterclockwise, rushing towards each other at an ever-increasing speed.

Ross emerged from the house and signaled for them to head back to the barn. He pulled up his shirt collar, protecting himself from the sandstorm that raged across the yard. He leapt off the porch and jogged towards his sister and two friends.

"We gotta get everyone indoors," he yelled over the whistling wind.

"Okay," Linda yelled back.

The kids turned around and hustled back towards the barn.

All at once, the heavens opened up. Hail the size of golf balls pelted the steel roof of the barn and bounced a foot off the ground, covering the yard in seconds with giant balls of ice. The cattle and the horses screamed.

"Ouch!" Hannah hollered, a hailstone hitting her in the head, just over her left eyebrow.

Johnny put an arm around her and guided her towards the barn.

"I'll go open up the loafing shed. You guys get Easter and the mares," Ross shouted.

Johnny and Linda nodded. Hannah held a hand to her face where a small red lump was forming over her left eye. Ross pushed past them and veered off into the loafing barn.

A great crash of thunder shook the earth. Lightning streaked across the sky, arcing from cloud to cloud in a series of horrific flashes. The hail was replaced by a driving sheet of rain. Rivers of water flowed through the front yard and meandered through the lower pasture, banks of ice pellets forming in its wake.

The storm increased in intensity, becoming as ferocious as a wounded lion. The wind shook the barn. Thunder peeled. Lightning flashed. It sounded like Niagara Falls during a flood.

A great, crashing BANG shook the earth. The cattle bolted, Merry Penny at the lead. They stampeded towards the barn, bawling and pushing in mass against the barn doors.

Pizzazz and Sal galloped up from the pasture in a wake of water and mud. The grey mare was frantic, her eyes rolling with fear. Sal snorted and lifted her tail over her rump, her hooves digging deep holes in the ground.

86

Claps of thunder echoed across the valley.

Pizzazz panicked! She careened past the cattle, saw the gate into Easter's paddock, and lifted herself off the ground and jumped over it. She sailed over the gate as if it wasn't there. Easter squealed in terror. Sal skidded to a stop, too short and stout to make such a leap, her chest slamming into the frail metal gate. The hinges gave way under her weight. Sal leaned harder and the metal gave way with a shriek. Sal burst through it in a frenzy.

Johnny and Ross yanked open the loafing shed doors and dove sideways as the cattle pushed past them. Ross turned and ran back into the barn to get out of the way. Johnny bounced off a cow and vaulted over the fence separating Easter's pen from the cattle yard when he saw Pizzazz jump the gate. He ran to intercept her, waving his arms over his head, trying to block the mare as she galloped headlong towards the outer gate, but she dodged around him. He realized that the mare wasn't going to stop and yelled at Hannah.

"Go get Ross. He's the only one who can control Pizzazz!"

The mare slipped sideways on a mound of ice and careened into the wire-framed outer gate. Her body crashed sideways against it. The metal screeched in protest. The fence pole holding the gate up snapped in half. The mare and the gate toppled to the ground.

"Ross! Help!" Hannah screamed at the top of her lungs as she ran into the stable. Linda brushed past her, two halters over her shoulder, her face white with fear.

Charlie Horse and Frosty whinnied shrilly from inside their stalls. Frosty reared, his hooves slashing at his stall door.

Ross bolted through the stable door, the cattle bawling and milling about in circles inside the barn behind him. He slammed the door shut and pulled down the wood brace. Hannah wheeled around, hot on Ross' heels. They skidded to a stop outside just as Pizzazz staggered to her feet and galloped past Johnny. Sal thundered past him as well and out into the yard. Easter screamed and galloped after the two mares.

"Easter!" Linda yelled helplessly as the filly darted past her. She burst into hysterical tears knowing that Easter's heart couldn't take this. She'd lose them both, Easter and the foal! "EASTER! Come back," she screamed again.

Tom and Mary McCloud ran out of the house, Will Sims and Mrs. Worthing scrambling along behind them. Waffles huddled deep inside his dog house, his body racked with shivers. Pizzazz galloped down the lane, heading for the highway, her hoof beats drowned out by the continuous crash of thunder. Easter took off behind the mare at a fast trot, her tail in the air, her fat belly bouncing up and down. The two horses disappeared into the driving rain. Sal galloped circles in the yard, water spewing out around her like a motorboat's wake.

Tom jumped off the porch and grabbed Sal's neck. Ross snuck around her far side and quickly slipped a halter over the terrified mare's head. Tom let go. Ross held on tight to the little Fjord as she bolted in a circle at the end of the lead line.

"Good girl, Sally," Tom cried out. "Hang on to her son!"

"Daddy!" Linda wailed. She ran towards her father, then felt the wind lift her up off her feet and toss her aside like a rag doll. She landed on her knees in the mud. Her father rushed to her side and picked her up off the ground.

Johnny pushed open the door to the stable. The wind was so strong that it took both he and Hannah to hold it open. Ross trotted Sal across the yard and into the barn. Tom cradled Linda in his arms and carried her into the stable. Johnny and Hannah let the barn door slam shut behind them.

"You girls stay here! Johnny, grab a couple of halters. Ross, you and Johnny come with me. We'll get the truck and go lookin' for the mares. We can't use the trailer in this wind," Tom hollered to be heard. The sound of the wind battering the barn's siding and the water cascading off the roof was deafening. "Let's hope they've run into someone else's yard. We'll get your mother to call all the neighbors!"

"Daddy! What's gonna happen to Easter?" Linda cried. She sniffled and wiped her tears on her shirt.

"We'll find her, Sweat Pea," her father said gently. He placed a firm hand on his daughter's shoulder. "You girls stay in the barn with the horses. You bein' here will help keep 'em calm. You don't go outside for any reason, you hear me?"

Hannah and Linda nodded.

The boys left the stable, disappearing into a driving sheet of rain, Hannah and Linda watching them go. The men barely made it to the truck without falling. The rain pelted down, driving against them with vicious fists. The yard was a quagmire of mud and debris.

Linda's mother waved from the porch, her blue apron was white with flour. Mrs. Worthing's hand was to her mouth and tears flowed down her cheeks, her apron also smudged with white. The plump woman's face was so red and her eyes so wild that she looked ripe for a heart attack. Mr. Sims draped a comforting arm over her shoulders and watched Tom and the boys skid their way out of the yard in the pickup truck.

"Call Doc Martin!" Tom shouted to his wife before he left.

Linda and Hannah went back into the stable. They filled the horses feed bins with hay and topped up their water. Sal put her head over Linda's shoulder and drew her in close to her chest, nibbling Linda's pockets, trying to make up for running away. Linda cuddled the old horse back, her face still streaked with tears. Hannah busied herself with Frosty and Charlie Horse, un-tacking the horses and giving them a quick rub down.

The wind abruptly quit howling! The clouds parted in the middle and the sun broke through. Linda ran outside and looked up.

"Do you think it's over?" Hannah asked from behind her.

"No! I think this is the eye of the storm. See how the clouds are swirling around the outer edges like they are. I think we might have a half hour or an hour though before it hits us again," Linda said.

"God. That was awful! I don't want to go through that again," Hannah moaned.

"Me neither, but it'll help the guys find Pizzazz and Easter," Linda added.

Hannah nodded. "I sure hope so."

"I'm gonna take Sal out and see if I can see their tracks," Linda said defiantly, whirling around.

"Your dad said to stay here!" Hannah exclaimed, her eyes wide with disbelief.

"I know, but I have to help find Easter. I don't want you to get in trouble so you stay here," Linda commanded. She placed her hands on her hips. Her eyes narrowed, daring Hannah to stop her. No one was going to keep her from trying to find Easter.

"Well. You aren't going without me!" Hannah answered, facing Linda. She could be as equally stubborn as her young friend.

"Fine!" Linda said.

"Fine!" Hannah responded.

The girls giggled.

"Well, you can't take Frosty and leave Charlie alone," Linda volunteered.

"No, I can't."

"We'll have to double on Sal. She won't mind if we just ride her bareback. Do you think you can stay on?" Linda asked, looking down at Hannah's prosthetic leg. Linda thought Hannah an excellent rider; Frosty was a real handful, but she doubted her friend had ever ridden bareback before.

"I'll stick! Don't you worry. If we find Easter and Pizzazz, you're going to have to lead them all home and you're gonna need help," Hannah said, lifting her chin proudly.

Linda grinned. "Let's go!"

Linda threw a bridle on Sal while Hannah dug up a rope halter from an old chest in the tack room. She slung it over her shoulder and followed Linda and Sal out into the back paddock.

"Mom will go nuts when she sees us leave. Move the busted gate, Hannah, and we'll mount back here," Linda pointed towards the mangled gate laying on the ground.

Hannah grabbed the steel frame and dragged the gate out of the way. She walked back over to where Linda had positioned Sal beside the old bathtub used as a water trough for the horses. Linda climbed up onto the tub's lip, steadied herself, then vaulted onto Sal's back.

"Come on, Hannah, we need to hurry before the storm starts up again," Linda squeaked.

Hannah jumped up onto the lip of the tub and climbed onto Sal's back. She sidled up to Linda and circled her arms around her waist.

Linda clucked to Sal and they were off!

Sal trotted down the lane quickly, the girls bouncing along on top of her. The mare arched her neck, snorted, and lifted her tail over her rump. Sal knew they were on an important mission.

"Linda, you come back here!" her mother wailed from the front porch.

"Linda, dear, stop!" cried Mrs. Worthing.

Waffles barked furiously from the front porch.

Linda kicked Sal into a canter. Hannah held on for dear life as the old mare shot forward with a little buck. Ole Man Levy opened his front door and stepped onto his front porch as the girls turned left on the highway in front of his house.

"What ya doin, ya silly fools?" he called, shielding his eyes from the sun's glare.

"Oh, noooo," Hannah groaned. Just one look from the old man could make her teeth chatter. Hannah felt sorry for the old fellow, but still kept her distance. He was dirty and smelled of tobacco.

"Have you seen Pizzazz or my new palomino, Mr. Levy?" Linda called, reining Sal to an abrupt halt.

"Yeahr...they jumped my fence and high-tailed it into the back forty. Leave it to yer pa, girl! I already called yer ma. That storm's fixin' ta open up agin!" The old man spat a wad of tobacco over the side of the porch.

"Thanks, Mr. Levy," Linda hollered and turned left, aiming Sal at the break in the old man's fence line. "Hold on, Hannah."

Hannah cradled herself against Linda's back and held on tight.

Linda pointed Sal's nose at the over-flowing ditch and put the boots to her. The mare reared and launched herself over the ditch, hooves tucked underneath her, her neck stretched out like a racehorse. She cleared the ditch, hurdling it like a pro. She galloped into the field with a great buck.

Hannah slipped sideways; Linda grabbed her arm and hauled her back into place. Hannah was two years older than Linda, but she was so petite that Linda was now two inches taller. She had no problem steadying Hannah.

"Look there!" Hannah pointed at the ground. Two sets of deep hoof prints led away across the pasture towards the forest.

Linda reined Sal around and galloped northwest in the direction of the tracks. The sky darkened once again. The clouds overhead swirled and churned. Lightning flickered between the clouds; thunder rumbled like a low bass drum. The wind started to pick up as the girls cantered across the open fields, the sun at their backs, the horizon before them as black and frightening as a castle's dungeon.

"Stop! Did you hear that?" Hannah cried out.

Linda tugged on Sal's reins. The mare slid to a halt. She snorted and whinnied. The horses' trail still led northwest, but Sal's whinny was greeted by a pair of answering calls from off to the west. The mares had doubled back, heading for home. Linda wheeled Sal around and let her trot forwards. The mare made a beeline for the gully in the distance.

The small gully dropped away before them. It was over-flowing from all the rain; brown water frothed and swirled, the banks slick and slippery. The hawthorn bushes and scrub alder that grew along the sides were awash with churning water. Pizzazz trotted in circles up and down the banks, her eyes wild with fear. Easter was stuck, belly deep in the dirty currents, her legs embedded in the muddy bottom. The mare squealed and screamed, the weight of the foal making it impossible for her to dig her way out of the trough she had fallen into.

"Easter!" Linda wailed.

Hannah and Linda jumped off Sal. Linda gave the reins to Hannah and ran, arms flailing, down the slope to her filly. Pizzazz reared and trotted over to Hannah. Hannah quickly slipped the rope halter onto the mare. Pizzazz nuzzled against her, clearly glad the girls had found her. Hannah knew instantly that neither she nor Linda would be able to get Easter out of the sink hole.

Linda waded into the icy water and cuddled up to Easter. The filly stopped screaming as soon as Linda reached her. The palomino's chest was thick with foam, some of it river scum, the rest was her own frothy sweat. Her legs looked as if they'd been cut off at the knees. Linda rubbed Easter's neck and put a hand on her belly. The foal kicked and thrashed; Easter's insides were taking a beating. The filly's breathing was labored; she struggled desperately for breath.

"Hannah! Go get help! There's no way that we can get her out of here by ourselves," Linda cried.

"Okay! I'm gonna take Pizzazz with me. I'll be back with your dad as fast as I can!" Hannah grabbed hold of Sal's bristly mane and swung her right leg into the air with all her might. It was hard to mount the mare since her prosthetic leg wasn't as balanced as the real thing. It took two tries, but she finally made it. She snatched up Pizzazz' lead line and reined Sal around, pointing her towards home.

The storm opened up with a driving force. Overhead, the clouds were revolving; they sped around, faster and faster.

"Hurry! It's a twister. Run for it!" Linda commanded, her voice raw with terror.

"What about you? You need to get out of there," Hannah yelled back, her voice breaking. Hannah's hands shook with fear. Sal snorted and pranced beneath her legs. Pizzazz danced sideways, almost tearing the rope out of Hannah's grasp. The wind picked up even more speed. Sal and Pizzazz reared, their eyes rolling, their nostrils inflamed with fear.

"I'm not leavin' Easter. Go! NOW!" Linda ordered.

Hannah nodded and kicked Sal forward. The Fjord jumped and dug her hooves into the muddy ground. She launched herself up the hill, setting a furious pace...even

95

Pizzazz had a hard time matching her stride as she leapt along beside her. Hannah urged the old mare on, holding onto the reins with one hand and Pizzazz with the other. She prayed to God that she could stay on. She had to get help or neither Easter nor Linda would survive the twister.

The funnel cloud formed and gathered strength overtop of the galloping horses. Hannah leaned forward, her heart pounding with absolute terror. She stopped worrying about Linda, realizing that she was in incredible danger and might not make it.

A loud roaring filled her ears; it threatened to shatter her eardrums. She wished that she could cover her ears to get away from the noise, but her hands were filled with leather reins and a lead rope. She thought her head was going to split wide open. She saw the tip of the twister bounce along the ground behind her, the funnel stretching from the earth to the heavens as far as her eyes could see.

The twister snarled and ripped Ole Man Levy's fence line out of the earth, tore trees out by the roots, and carried everything up into its swirling black mouth. Hannah screamed, her voice lost in the roaring of the wind. The twister bounced along behind her as if propelled forward by an unseen hand, then it bore down on her and the galloping horses!

# Chapter Eight

## Ole Man Levy

Linda watched Hannah gallop away on Sal, Pizzazz leaping into the air beside her. Overtop of the gully, she saw the funnel cloud touch down and heard the ripping whine as it tore the forest to shreds. Terror seized her heart in a vicious grip. She knew she was going to die; any minute, the twister would bounce down the hill and rip Easter and her out of the slew and carry them off into its belly. She screamed, closed her eyes, wrapped her arms around the palomino's neck and held on tight. Within minutes, the twister moved east towards the river, leaving Linda and Easter to their fate.

Linda shivered and huddled closer to the filly. The water roiled around them. Her whole body was racked with tremors as was Easter's. Her fingers and feet had gone numb; the water was freezing. She stood there, holding onto Easter, her blues lips praying that Hannah would return with help soon. She didn't know how much longer that she could hang on. The current was picking up speed. A large branch slammed into her back causing a bolt of pain to streak up her spine.

"God, help us, please!" Linda begged through chattering teeth, her blond hair plastered to her face. The roar of the wind was deafening. She gritted her teeth. It felt like her eardrums were going to burst; they throbbed painfully.

Rain pelted down on top of them. Linda snuggled her face down into the filly's mane. The raindrops were so large and coming down so hard that they stung her skin.

She looked up and saw a large sheet of green aluminum fly by. The wind carried it along as if it was a small leaf. It disappeared over the ridge.

She thought she heard a truck door slam, but the sound was carried away by the storm. A fierce tremor gripped her and she fell backwards into the water. Easter whinnied and reached her head down. Linda grabbed hold of her halter and pulled herself back up. She sputtered and spat out a mouthful of foul tasting water. It left her feeling like she hadn't brushed her teeth in a week.

Linda noticed that the foal had stopped kicking inside Easter's belly. She cried, her tears mixing with the rain that ran down her cheeks. She suspected that they were too late. The foal had probably died! The water was too cold and the filly's flight had probably ruptured something inside her. All Linda could wish for now was that the filly was strong enough to hold on until they were rescued.

"Linda!" a shaky voice called.

Linda looked up and saw two figures scrambling down the bank through a thick veil of rain. At first, she thought she was dreaming. She was so cold that she found that she couldn't even think any more. She had now lost all feeling in her lower body.

The roaring of the twister had disappeared and the rain eased off just a little bit. She realized that there really were two people slipping and sliding the last few feet down the hill towards her. It wasn't her imagination. Easter nickered under her breath, a sad sound that filled Linda's heart with despair. The filly was exhausted.

"Good gawd!" the old man muttered, surveying the situation. Rain dripped off his John Deere cap in a steady stream. His dark oilskin coat glistened with water droplets and his face was white and pasty, his thin lips pursed with worry.

Hannah ran past him and jumped into the water. She wrapped a woolen blanket around Linda's shoulders. The old man spun on his heel and jogged back up the hill.

Linda tugged the blanket up around her neck, grateful for the small warmth it offered. She noticed that Hannah's blue eyes were bloodshot and swollen with tears.

"S'okay," Linda said bravely, her voice thin and reedy. "You brought Ole Man Levy?"

"He was the closest," Hannah whispered, hugging her friend. "There wasn't any time. The twister was right over top of Johnny's house!"

Ole Man Levy came back down the hill with a heavy bundle of ropes. He had fastened one end of the thick rope to the bumper of his old Dodge pickup. He waded into the swirling creek and quickly made a sling around the filly's belly, careful to keep the rope tucked in behind her front legs, away from her pregnant belly. He snapped a lead line to the filly's halter and climbed back onto the bank.

"Can ya drive, girl?" he asked Hannah.

"I can drive a tractor," she squeaked.

The old man nodded, a shower of water falling off his cap. His skin was as pale as death, but his eyes shone with a ferocious light.

"Not much different," he said, dryly. "Put 'er in 'Drive'. Keep yer foot on the brake until I signals, then take it off and press the gas pedal on the right real slow. As soon as the filly's on the bank, hit the brake and reverse to take some tension off the rope. Ya got it?"

"Yes, sir," Hannah replied. She gave Linda one more hug and scrambled back up the bank, slipping and sliding all the way.

"Come on, dear. Out with ya," the old man reached under Linda's arms and dragged her onto the bank. "Go sit over yonder and let's see if we can save this horse of yours."

Linda sat huddled on the sodden grass. Easter lifted her head and checked to make sure that Linda was still there. Ole Man Levy gave the filly a gentle pat, trying to reassure her. The palomino's body shook violently with seizures.

"Whoa, girl. We'll get ya out of 'ere," he crooned.

Easter accepted the old man's words and touch with great tolerance.

Ole Man Levy tightened the grip on the lead rope and leaned backwards. He lifted a hand and waved it over his head, signaling Hannah to drive forward.

Hannah put the truck in gear. The brake lights shone red, then went off as the truck slowly pulled forward. The rope sling went taught.

"Come on , Easter. Push!" Linda yelled. She stood up, her shoulders hunched over, and dropped the blanket in the mud. She leaned around the old man and snatched up the end of the rope. Ole Man Levy smiled slightly and grunted.

The filly strained her neck forward and lifted her right front leg out of the muck. It came out of the mud with a deep slurping and sucking sound. She groaned with the effort. The mud sucked at her belly; it clung to her with a life of its own. The old Dodge coughed out a cloud of blue-black smoke. The tires spun. Hannah pressed down on the gas pedal and the truck jumped ahead. The filly grunted and reared, her hind legs thrashing in the mucky water.

"Come on, little girl, heave!" the old man shouted, sitting back with all his weight, Linda doing the same behind him. They pulled and tugged on the line together.

Easter screamed and leapt out of the mud with the last of her strength. She stumbled onto the grass and collapsed on the ground, her sides heaving, her breathing ragged. Ole Man Levy hollered and waved a hand over his head. Hannah reversed the truck as she was told to do. The rope's tension was released and the sling around the filly's belly sagged. Hannah slammed the truck into 'Park', jumped out of the cab, and slid down the hill on her bottom.

Ole Man Levy quickly cut the ropes that bound the horse. He whispered quietly to the filly as Linda cradled her head in her lap. Easter's nostrils were red and inflamed. She snorted and heaved, struggling for breath.

Hannah snatched the wool blanket from the ground and threw it back over Linda's shoulders just as another truck came skidding to a halt at the crest of the hill. Tom, Johnny and Ross jumped out and ran wildly down the hill, arms wind-milling, feet sliding on the slippery slope.

"Oh thank, God!" Tom declared. "I thought I'd lost you, Sweet Pea."

"Have ya got some tarps and blankets in that truck of yers, Tommy?" Ole Man Levy asked Tom.

"Aye!" Tom answered.

"What about a respirator?" he asked.

"No," answered Tom.

"Go up ta ma truck, boy, and get the oxygen tank and tubing from behind the seat," Ole Man Levy commanded.

"I'll get 'em," Ross said and darted back up the hill to the Dodge. He ran back, his arms filled with a large canvas tarp, a fleecy horse blanket and a small rusty oxygen tank.

"Right. Throw the tarp over the filly. She's shakin' somethin' fierce. I'm gonna go in and tug the foal out. It's the only way to make sure we can save the filly," Ole Man Levy suggested.

Tom nodded. "Yeah. I figured as much. I expect the foal's gone anyway."

Linda sobbed and stroked Easter's blaze. The filly lifted her head and looked at the old man with trusting eyes.

"By Gawd, we'll save this girl for ya," the old man patted Linda on the shoulder. Linda was surprised that

102

his words made her feel better. Ole Man Levy certainly seemed to know what to do.

The sound of the wind slowed to a soft whoosh and the rain settled into a light drizzle. The water in the gully rushed by them, the soggy fields unable to contain any more liquid. A frothy brown scum piled itself around the flooded bushes along the creek bed. The temperature dropped and a light ground fog formed over the water, drifting across the gully like a thin veil of smoke.

"What can I do?" Johnny asked, his breath a frosty steam in front of his face.

"You go stand with Hannah, but get another blanket outa ma truck for the young 'un here first. She's gonna get pneumonia if we don't get 'er warmed up," the old man said.

Johnny rushed off and came back with another grey blanket which he placed over Linda's shaking form. She smiled and nodded her thanks.

The filly's breathing started to return to normal as her temperature rose. Her ears revolved this way and that, listening to Ole Man Levy as he spoke soothing words to her.

Ross and his father joined the old man at the back of the filly. The old man lifted the canvas tarp. "The foal's already comin' on its own," he said.

The men watched as first the front legs and then the head appeared. At that point, the filly ran out of steam and couldn't push the foal out any further.

"Easy, girl," the old man crooned, getting down in the mud and gently pulling the foal the rest of the way out of the filly. The birth sac popped out with a soft whoosh.

The foal was covered in a thin, white membrane. Ole Man Levy broke it with this fingers. The foal was white and spindly with a small black smudge on the top of its head. Its eyes were closed and its chest didn't move.

"Damn!" Tom swore. "We were all prayin' for this little one."

"It's real pretty too," Ross muttered quietly.

"Don't give up yet, boys," Ole Man Levy said. "Hand me the respirator."

Ross placed the tank and tubing at the old man's feet. Ole Man Levy bent down and cleaned the mucous out of the foal's nose and mouth. He hooked the tubing to the oxygen tank, opened the valve on top, and let out a huge sigh of relief when he heard a soft hiss coming from the end of the tube. He didn't know if there was any oxygen left; it had been years since he needed it and he was actually taking the tank to be disposed of. That was why it was in the truck in the first place. He placed one end of the tube down the foal's nose, attached the plastic ventilator bag and gave the chest a few light compressions. The foal's chest rose as the oxygen was forced into its lungs. The old man squeezed the plastic bag several times in a steady rhythm, waited for the bag to expand, then compressed it again. The foals eyes remained shut. The old man started muttering to himself. All at once, the foal opened its eyes and inhaled a deep breath.

"Alright!" everyone exclaimed at once.

"Give me that blanket, pronto," the old man said to Ross.

Ross picked up the horse blanket and gave it to the old man. He gingerly wrapped the foal in the soft fleecy blanket. The foal struggled a couple of times, then let the old man hug it to his body.

"Help me get it inta the truck. We gotta get it outa the rain," Ole Man Levy said as Tom McCloud helped him to his feet.

"What about Easter?" Linda whined. "We can't leave her!"

"Well. We gotta hope that she's tough enough to get up now. If she can't, I'm afraid that we'll have to just worry about savin' the foal now," the old man said honestly.

Linda shivered, great sobs of grief tearing through her chest. She couldn't bear the thought of losing Easter. Johnny and Hannah helped her to her feet, one on each arm. "Easter. You gotta fight!" she said to the filly.

The filly snorted and struggled to sit up, her legs thrashing about wildly. Johnny pulled the tarp off her. Steam rose off the horse's back in a great wave. She stank of blood, sweat and river scum. The filly whinnied, a sick sound that made everyone's stomach churn. There didn't seem like there was much hope for the palomino now.

"Come on, Easter," Hannah and Linda said together.

"Yeah, come on, Easter, you can do it," Johnny urged, walking around behind the horse and grabbing a tight hold of her tail like he had done before.

Linda dropped the lead line, her hands too cold to hold onto it anymore. Hannah picked it up off the ground and held on tight.

The men carried the foal up the hill. Ross jumped into the back of his father's pickup. He sat down at the rear of the cab as the old man and his father lifted the foal into the truck bed. He cradled the foal against his body for added warmth. Easter watched them go. She screamed, a shrill sound that shattered the air and tore at the heart.

"Come on, Easter. You don't want them to take away your baby, do you?" Hannah yelled at the horse.

Easter screamed again and lunged upwards. Johnny let go of her tail and jumped out of the way. Hannah sat back, yanking on the lead line. The palomino staggered to her feet.

Linda cheered.

The horse snorted and tried to gallop up the hill after her baby, but she staggered sideways, almost falling. Johnny snatched up her tail and swung wildly from side to side in the opposite direction of her fall, trying to help Easter stay balanced. He let go, stumbled forward, then righted himself once again. The palomino dug deep into her reserves of strength and fumbled her way up the hill with Hannah pulling on her head and Johnny pushing her from behind. Linda struggled up the hill after them. They all stopped at the top of the grade, their chests heaving and their cheeks flushed.

"You know, Linda," Johnny gasped, leaning forward, his hands on his thighs. "You know what I never thought to ask you?"

"What?" Linda asked breathlessly, her shoulders slumped with weariness.

"I reckon I should'a asked just once if this horse of yours kicks before I started tuggin' and pushin' on her hind end," Johnny croaked.

Linda and Hannah burst into a fit of uncontrollable giggles. Johnny smiled up at them.

"Yeah, you should'a," Hannah snorted, patting Johnny on the back.

Johnny straightened up and grinned, his eyes dancing with mirth.

"Well, I guess we know now that she doesn't, but I wouldn't recommend that you try that with Pizzazz or Frosty," Linda added. She grinned. "Phew, I feel like I've climbed Mount Everest!"

"Me too," Hannah puffed.

Easter grunted and surged forward, letting the kids know it was time to move.

Tom put the tailgate down on the truck so that Easter could see and smell her foal in the truck bed. Linda, Johnny and Hannah climbed onto the tailgate, but Linda's father insisted that Linda ride in the front to get warm.

"But, Dad," Linda whined.

"Hurry up, Linda, you're wasting precious time," her father said angrily.

Linda shut her mouth, looked at the state of her shivering horse and foal and leapt into the truck beside her father.

Ole Man Levy led the way back to the highway and drove to the McClouds' farm with Tom following close behind him. They drove slowly, not wanting to make Easter's journey any worse than it already was. Ole Man Levy had told Tom privately on their way up the hill that it would take a miracle for either the mother or the foal to survive.

As they drove into the yard, Mary shouted from the porch, "Doc Martin is on the way!"

Mrs. Worthing and Mr. Sims darted down the stairs after the two trucks. Mary ran back into the house to get the kids a change of clothes and to put the coffee on. It was clear it was going to be a long night.

# Chapter Nine

## Of Miracles and Easter Bonnets

The twister had disappeared with the rush of cold air coming down from the north-west. A cold drizzle fell from the low slung clouds. The day was dank and sullen, the sky a depressing grey. There was no twilight and darkness fell quickly.

Doc Martin came roaring into the yard in his Chevy, tires spinning, mud spewing in every direction. The big Chevy's headlights illuminated the barn door where Mr. Sims was standing, ringing his hands, his face as downcast as the gloomy weather.

"How are they doing?" Doc Martin asked, jumping out of his truck.

"Easter is doing better than expected, but the foal isn't fairing all that well," Mr. Sims croaked.

Doc Martin nodded, snatched up his large black medical bag from the front seat and brushed wordlessly past Mr. Sims. The two men walked into the stable. The crowd standing outside Easter's stall was hushed. The filly looked as stricken as the people that gathered around her. She nickered sadly at Doc Martin, the palomino already having developed a bond with the vet.

Doc Martin gave her a very quick look over, satisfied the horse did indeed appear to be breathing evenly and was not in distress. He was amazed that she was still standing, given the phone conversation he had with Tom McCloud an hour earlier. The roads to and from River Bend were closed due to flooding and he had to back track and come in from the west just to get to the McClouds. One glance at the pitifully helpless foal lying on the ground swaddled in blankets made his heart sink.

"How long has it been now?" he asked Ole Man Levy who was squatting down at the foal's head, monitoring its breathing. The old man had kept the oxygen tank and respirator handy in case they needed it again. Doc Martin was pleased to see that.

"Near an hour and a half since the little 'un was born. I had ta pull her the last of the way out; the poor filly was done fer," he said, shaking his head. "We've been keeping her warm and dry. The tank here is almost empty so it's a good thing she's bin able to breathe on her own."

"Good," Doc Martin grunted. He pulled out his stethoscope and pulled back the blanket. The foal lifted its head and looked at him through piercing blue eyes.

"I'll be damned!" the vet said. "Interesting looking little filly, isn't she?"

The little filly tried to suck on his fingers as he placed the stethoscope on her chest and listened to her heartbeat. He proceeded to give her a full exam.

"I told Ross that Easter was gonna have a filly, didn't I?" Linda said half-heartedly.

"You called it," the vet agreed.

110

"Have you ever seen anything like her, Doc?" Tom asked. "I don't ever recall seeing a white horse with blue eyes and a black cap of hair on its head like that before?"

Doc Martin shook his head. "No, can't say as I have!"

"Well, we can always call her 'the Mad Hatter'," Linda's mother joked weakly, trying to boost everyone's spirits.

"Mom!" Linda exclaimed. "Don't name her until we know she's gonna be okay. It's bad luck!"

"Okay, Sweet Pea. Take it easy," her father chided her gently.

Linda sat cross-legged on the ground beside the foal, right next to Ole Man Levy. She had been praying fervently all during the ride back home and during her vigil in the stall that the foal would make it. Her mother had a terrible time trying to get her to come in the house to change into some dry sweat pants and sweat shirt; in the end, Linda changed clothes in the tack room. Her black fleecy pants were covered in cedar shavings.

Easter put her head down and nuzzled her foal, then picked up a strand of Linda's hair and began to chew on it. Linda gently pulled her hair out of the filly's mouth.

Doc Martin finished the exam and looked at Tom. Tom, Linda and Ole Man Levy were the only ones in the stall with him. Ross, Johnny, Hannah, Linda's mother, Mrs. Worthing and Mr. Sims clustered around the stall door, anxiously awaiting the vet's verdict.

"Well, her knees and hocks are filled with fluid...see how they're all swollen at the joints? That's quite common when you have to give the mare a helping hand by pulling the foal out. She's got a bacterial infection from the creek water so we'll treat her for that as well. The next

111

few hours are critical. She's soaked the blanket with diarrhea; get rid of that immediately. I expect she's also got an ulcerated stomach from the filly's seizures. All told, this little girl's got a big fight ahead of her!"

"What are her chances, Doc?" Tom asked.

"Well, Tom, this filly shouldn't even be alive in my professional opinion, but here she lies. Because of that, I'm not even going to hazard a guess," Doc Martin confessed.

"Our Easter has always been a strong girl," Mr. Sims said, tears forming at the corners of his eyes. "I wouldn't expect any less of her babies."

"Aye. She's tough as an old billy goat, our Easter. Might be a gid thing that the wee un's da was a wild mustang too," Mrs. Worthing offered.

"I expect yer right on that, missus," said Ole Man Levy.

Mrs. Worthing blushed, her eyes sparkling.

"I'm going to give the filly and the foal a shot of antibiotics to fight off the infection. I'm also going to leave you some Visorbin. It's a concentrated vitamin B complex; it looks and tastes like green apples so the foal should like it. I'm also going to give you some antibiotic paste that I want you to keep giving to the foal. Try and help it to its feet in about an hour to see if it can nurse. If not, you'll need to collect the colostrum from Easter and start bottle feeding the filly every hour," the vet said, everyone present hanging on his every word.

"I'll look after gettin' the colostrum," Ross volunteered.

"Right. Keep me posted," Doc Martin said as his pager went off. "I can see that it's going to be a long day for me. Thank God that twister didn't last more than a few minutes. You were lucky that you didn't lose your house or barn, Johnny!"

"Yes, sir," Johnny nodded. "I already talked to my folks. Can I get a lift home? Dad says we've got some cattle down."

Doc Martin nodded. "I'll be stopping at your place next."

"Is it okay to leave Charlie here, Mr. McCloud? I'll come get him later," Johnny asked.

"Come get him in the morning, son," Tom offered. "Your parents have their hands full and they need you!"

"Yes, sir," Johnny replied.

Doc Martin gave Easter a pat, readied a syringe of antibiotics and gave her a shot in the neck. The palomino didn't flinch. She looked down as he removed the needle and nuzzled the doctor's arm. He smiled, then administered antibiotics to the foal.

"Keep the foal's rear end clean and give Easter a bath, especially around the udder. I want all that swamp water off of her," the vet added, while packing up his bag.

"I can look after that," Mr. Sims said, his face brightening at finally being able to offer some help.

"Doc, I'm gonna send you off with some coffee and fresh baking that Mrs. Worthing and I have been fixing since early this morning and I won't hear any arguments about it," Linda's mother commented, her voice stern.

"I won't argue with you, Mary," Doc Martin said. He chuckled. "I'll tell my wife to phone you when I've gained twenty pounds and she has to let my pants out."

113

"I'm sure she'll understand." Linda's mother laughed merrily.

Mrs. Worthing's spirits lifted too; this was her territory and she understood it. The two women hustled the vet off to the house. He left carrying a satchel of cookies, cinnamon buns, a chunk of cheddar cheese and freshly made biscuits, plus a couple of apples and a steaming mug of coffee.

Ross and Mr. Sims went up to the house and brought back four buckets of warm water. Ross placed two outside the stall door. Mr. Sims carried the other two into the stall and bathed Easter, just like the vet ordered. The palomino nickered and cuddled up to her former owner, but never took her eyes off her baby. Mr. Sims stroked her neck and sang to her softly. Easter sighed, her muscles visibly relaxing, enjoying both the warm bath and the song.

The foal squealed and licked its lips. It kicked out with its hind feet, not wanting the blanket on top of it anymore. The little filly's fur was now dry; her pelt was cottony soft. Her eyes were starting to grow a little brighter and more alert as the antibiotics started to take effect.

"Is she okay?" Hannah asked worriedly, leaning over the stall door. For the first time, she wasn't afraid of Ole Man Levy anymore. She realized that both Easter and her foal would be dead right now if it wasn't for him. She had no idea that the old man had that much skill, forgetting that he had been a rancher once too. After his wife's passing, Ole Man Levy had given up on life and allowed his grief to turn itself into a bitter hatred for everything and everyone. If it breathed, he hated it. If it talked, he despised it, or that was what Hannah thought.

"Aye, it's normal, child," Ole Man Levy said. "Sometimes foals when they're born are so still that ya think they're gonners. They get tired, ya see. It's a tough thing, being born; it takes the stuffin' outa some of 'em. This little 'un, we already know'd was in trouble."

The foal lifted its head and poked its nose into Linda's ear. She giggled and pulled away. The foal opened its mouth and let out a shrill whinny. Easter immediately broke away from Mr. Sims, walked over to her baby, and lowered her head. She nuzzled the foal and started to clean its face.

"Good girl, Easter. She's a beauty, your little girl," Linda told the mare.

Easter snorted and continued to stand over Linda and the foal.

Ole Man Levy stood up with the help of Tom McCloud. "I guess I'm a long ways short of being considered 'spry' anymore," he joked.

"I don't know what we'd have done without you, Sam," Tom confessed. "We all owe you our thanks."

"Sam?" Linda and Hannah mouthed to each other. It never occurred to either of the girls that Ole Man Levy would have a first name.

The old man guffawed. "Well, don't go thankin' me yet, that foal's a long way from being outa the woods." The old man lifted the small silver oxygen tank. "Help me get this outa here," he said to Tom. "Keep it by the door, case ya need it."

"Can I go and fetch anyone some coffee and treats?" Hannah asked sheepishly. "I'd like to help and I can't think of anything else to do."

"Now I can think of a few things," Ole Man Levy teased, placing a finger underneath his chin. "Well, let's see, you've got horses that want brushin' and feedin' stalls ta clean, cattle ta water and feed. Oh, and have ya called yer own ma yet?"

"Oh, no, I haven't," Hannah cried, her face stricken. "I don't even know if the twister hit our house!"

Hannah wheeled around on one heel and ran for Linda's house. She knocked over one of Ross' buckets of warm water in the process; it spilled down the aisle.

"Hey!" Ross called after her. "That was for cleanin' up the foal, not the barn!"

The three men in the stable laughed out loud. Ross turned to look at them, his face red, then he too broke out laughing.

The foal, its head and two front hooves still in Linda's lap, started to struggle.

"Owww! I think I need some help down here," Linda squeaked.

Her father rushed over and squeezed in against the wall. He lifted the foal up gently so that his daughter could wiggle her way out from underneath it.

The foal let out a mewling cry and tried to push itself up onto its spindly legs. All four legs wobbled and splayed sideways. The foal swayed this way and that. Tom placed both arms under its belly to keep it from falling. Linda held up the little filly's head. The foal's black skull cap wavered from side to side like a plate on

116

the end of a juggler's stick as the foal tipped sideways. Linda giggled uncontrollably.

With Tom still holding it up, the foal tried to walk over to its mother. Easter waited patiently while bit by bit, her baby skidded and staggered across the stall floor, licking her lips and bleating softly. When she reached her mother, the little filly nipped her belly playfully. The filly reached underneath Easter's stomach and found what she was looking for. She slurped and poked her head against her mother's tummy, drinking up the milk.

"Yeah!" everyone cheered.

"Well, that thar's a good sign," Ole Man Levy muttered.

Ole Man Levy, Ross and Mr. Sims all shook hands, smiles on their faces and twinkles in their eyes. Tom was left, bent over, holding the filly up as she fed. The foal stood there, legs out, thin neck stretched forwards, her short broom-like tail flicking back and forth with every drink she took.

The ladies came back from the house carrying trays full of food, a pot of hot tea, a thermos of coffee, and cups and napkins for everyone. They all shouted with glee at the sight of the nursing foal.

"Can I offer ya a wee drop of tea?" Mrs. Worthing cooed to Ole Man Levy.

"That would be right nice of yer, ma'am," Ole Man Levy blushed.

"So, are you gonna name her now?" Hannah asked Linda through a mouthful of peanut butter cookie. She finished the cookie, licked the crumbs from her lips and wiped her fingers on her jeans. She had talked to her mother, who had been frantic for hours wondering if her daughter was okay. Her father had been more than a little angry on the phone talking to her, but he finally calmed down once he realized she really was fine. Both her parents had said that they would be up to the farm shortly to pick her up.

"We can't just call her 'it' anymore," said Mary, "and I do like The Mad Hatter idea."

Linda sighed.

The foal had enough to drink. Easter turned her head and sniffed her little girl. Tom and his daughter helped the foal to lay back down with a splattering of legs, blankets and cedar shavings. The foal sat up, tucked its head down, its nuzzle resting on top of one leg, yawned and closed its eyes.

"Well, we missed Easter by a day," Linda said sadly.

"You can't have everything, Sweet Pea," her father quipped, amused, leaning against the stall door and accepting a cup of coffee from his wife.

"How about Miracle?" Hannah offered. "What about that?"

There were murmurs of agreement; that was a good one.

"I think we should call her Spot!" Ross laughed.

"She's not a dog, Ross! I know what her name is gonna be," Linda said heavily, rolling her eyes at her brother. Sometimes she thought her big brother was daft; she liked that word and didn't think Mrs. Worthing would mind her using it. Linda paused a moment. She looked around and saw everyone nodding in agreement, then over to Easter and back to the little white foal with the round black splotch between its ears. "I guess that

118

we're just gonna have to call her, Bonnet...you know, Easter Bonnet!"

Everyone roared with laughter.

"That's a mighty fine name, Sweet Pea," her father answered.

"Bonnet! I love it," her mother cooed.

"A right fine handle too. I like it, Easter Bonnet," Ole Man Levy nodded and took a sip of tea.

Linda threw her arms around the little filly's neck and hugged her to her chest. The filly opened one blue eye, looked up at Linda, chewed on her lip for a moment, then went back to sleep. Being born was exhausting!

# Chapter Ten

## *An Easter to Remember*

Phones were ringing off the hook in River Bend, Knob Hill and Cold River; everyone was talking about the twister and the amazing birth of the filly now known as Easter Bonnet. The McClouds, the Joes and the Storeys couldn't keep up with the calls or the gossip. No one could believe that Ole Man Levy had delivered the foal! The only two people in town who weren't surprised were Momma Lotham and Bill Johansen. Bill and Momma Lotham had exchanged a wink and a smile when they heard the news.

The twister had destroyed the Joes' secondary hay barn and toppled their grain silo, but thankfully it turned east before hitting anything else. They lost all of their fencing too, but no lives were lost. Hannah's barn, the one that the townsfolk had built for her two years earlier, had been leveled. Frosty would have been killed for sure if she and Johnny hadn't ridden over to the McClouds and been stranded there by the storm. In less than fifteen minutes, the twister had done incredible damage!

It ripped trees up by the roots and tossed them around like matchsticks. Huge cedar and spruce trees sat in the middle of plowed fields, their branches reaching up to the heavens as if asking for mercy. The northern section of the forest looked like it had been hit by a meteor; the twister had cut a huge swath of destruction down the center of it. It just missed Pumpkin Alley and the old trapper's cabin. Deep black holes filled with scummy water now existed where once ancient spruce trees had stood. There was no fencing to be seen anywhere from Ole Man Levy's farm to the river; the land lay as open as it had been before the pioneers came.

The Athabasca River was filled with debris: tree limbs, tree trunks, building material, and even an aluminum shed floated down the river! The waterline was only five feet under the bridge overhang so River Bend's bridge and train trestle were closed until the water went down, shutting River Bend off to the east. The sound of the muddy water was deafening. Tree trunks floating downstream slammed into the trestle and split in two or were caught against the steel girders, creating small dams around the rusty iron beams. Highway crews watched helplessly from the shore as the bridge and trestle's footings shook violently from the pounding they were receiving.

Power was out all over the northwest. It didn't worry folks much in River Bend and Cold River as most farms had generators. They always lost power during winter blizzards and were prepared for it.

Several buildings in River Bend had lost sections of their roofs, including the church. Pastor Smith was going to cancel Easter Service until Tom and Mary McCloud offered to host it at their farm.

On Easter morning, Mother Nature cooperated. The sun came out and temperatures soared. The pastures sparkled, the fields turning a luscious green. The trees left standing in the forest were budding and the crocus beneath them were blooming. Barn swallows darted in and out of the stable, cheeping and chirping, their beaks filled with twigs and tufts of hair to line their nests with. Hundreds of starlings and sparrows swarmed over the dark fields, the mud finally starting to dry up.

Tables were brought in from the church and covered with festively colored plastic table cloths. Power was restored and urns of coffee percolated while pots of tea brewed. Wives, mothers, and daughters had been up most of the night making sandwiches and baking treats. The tables were lined with the results: pinwheel tuna and egg salad sandwiches, brownies, lemon tarts, apple pies, pickled beans, dill pickles, lemon meringue pies, everything that one could imagine. Mrs. Worthing had baked a carrot cake and wrote "Happy Birthday Easter" on it. The women of River Bend loved a good church social.

Chairs were lined up in rows in the McClouds' back yard, apple trees bursting into leaf above them. Ross and Waffles herded the Limousin cattle down to the bottom pasture so that they wouldn't disturb the service. The cattle grazed happily on the sweet meadow grasses. Pizzazz and Sal were allowed in the front paddock beside the house. Sal leaned over the fence and snuggled up to kids, many of whom couldn't resist pinching carrots off the vegetable trays on the dinner table and feeding them to the fat little Fjord.

Easter and her foal were stabled in the barn, away from prying eyes. Linda stayed with her, only venturing into the house briefly to change into her dress.

Few had seen the little white filly as Doc Martin forbade any visitors to the farm until he felt Bonnet was strong enough to stand the attention. The filly's recovery was remarkable, but Bonnet was still on antibiotics and her health was delicate. Doc Martin didn't want anything to go wrong. He would allow her to be brought out for a few minutes during the service, but everyone had been warned not to touch the mare or her foal.

Johnny and Hannah kept watch at the stable while Linda was gone, scooting away numerous curious children. Johnny looked grand in his grey suit, his black hair gleaming. He tried to look gruff as he stood guard in front of the barn doors, but kept bursting into laughter every time he had to carry a kicking and screaming toddler back across the yard to a weary-eyed mother. Most of the time, Hannah stood close by his side, feeling awkward in her pale blue dress and grey suede boots because the top six inches of her prosthetic leg were clearly visible. Many of the younger kids stopped to gawk. She knew they were just interested, but their stares made her blush.

"Well folks," Pastor Smith called to the gathering. "Welcome one and all, especially our two visitors from Knob Hill, Mr. Sims and Mrs. Worthing. I'd also like to welcome Sherry and Jennifer Arneson from Cold River. It's good to see you at Service too, Samuel Levy!"

The townsfolk gathered up their children and took their seats. Everyone was dressed in their Sunday best: men and boys wore ties, starched shirts and woolen suits, while ladies and girls wore dresses and sported Easter bonnets. The bonnets were fastened tightly around their chins with brightly colored ribbons and had fresh or silk flowers pinned to the sides or on top. The townsfolk nodded a greeting to Mr. Sims, Mrs. Worthing, Sherry and her daughter, then cast curious glances Ole Man Levy's way. He hadn't been seen at church in at least ten years.

"Many of us owe our thanks today! It has been quite a difficult winter. Hardships have been great this year, but through it all, we have received many small, and some not so small, miracles," joked the pastor.

The crowd chuckled. Tom picked up his wife's hand and smiled at her. Jim Storey, Hannah's father, put his arm around his wife's shoulder and gave it a squeeze. The Joes nodded and smiled. Mrs. Joe's face was beaming; for the first time in eleven years, she didn't feel like an outsider in River Bend. Mr. Sims' eyes grew filmy and Mrs. Worthing put a steadying hand on his knee. Ole Man Levy sat beside Mrs. Worthing looking stiff and uncomfortable in his brown pinstriped suit. He kept glancing nervously at Mrs. Worthing. It seemed that he had finally met his match.

"As you know, the Joes have lost their hay barn and all their silage. If anyone can spare any feed until their pasture grows in, that would be appreciated. The Storeys have lost the small stable that we built for them a couple of years ago. The McClouds have offered to stable Hannah's pony until a new one can be built. Fencing has to be replaced all the way from the Johansen farm to the river. The flooding and closure of the bridge forced many to stay home today, but I know their hearts are with us. We can only hope that we don't lose the bridge or the trestle with the river the way it is. We were lucky, folks! No one was killed and no livestock was lost!"

"Amen to that, Pastor," shouted Momma Lotham, her ample bottom falling over both sides of her chair as she fanned her sweaty face with her bonnet. Mom's Restaurant was closed for the first time in history because the cook lived on the far side of the river.

There were murmurs of consent throughout the congregation. Jim Storey reached over and shook Tom McCloud's hand. Jennifer climbed off her mother's lap and plopped herself down on Mrs. Joe's, then proceeded to tell Mrs. Joe all about her pony, Snowflake, and how it was her mother that introduced Easter to Linda McCloud. Mrs. Joe listened with rapt attention. Sherry flashed her a look of apology, but Mr. Joe grinned and winked at her, knowing that Jennifer had just made his wife's day.

"The one truly remarkable miracle, I think, is the birth of young Linda McCloud's filly, Bonnet. I say a miracle, not just because she survived a hard delivery, freezing rain and a twister, but because her mother, Easter, was able to carry a foal to term despite her young age." Pastor Smith smiled, a large toothy grin, his brown eyes sparkling, the sun bouncing off his bald head.

At the mention of Easter's name, Linda pushed open the door of the stable and led her mare and foal out into the yard. The little foal frolicked on wobbly legs beside its mother. Bonnet snorted and reared as the table cloths fluttered under a light breeze. The filly's white coat glistened in the sunshine. Easter walked, head in the air, tail swishing from side to side, obviously proud of her little one.

There was a series of "Ooohhhs" and "Ahhhhs".

"She's gorgeous!" Momma Lotham exclaimed. "Look at those blue eyes!"

"Oh, I can't wait to paint her," Hannah's mother gushed.

"Keep the little ones seated, folks!" Pastor Smith laughed as a dozen youngsters tried to bolt from their seats. They were grabbed instantly by the arm or around the waist by their parents. There were squeals of delight and disappointment.

"Take a good look," Doc Martin commanded, standing up in the front row and glaring at those seated around him, "because no one is to bother that foal until the doctor says so!" The vet then burst into a fit of giggles.

"Better listen," Pastor Smith crowed. "I don't think anyone here wants to anger the only vet for fifty miles."

Doc Martin's wife grabbed him and hauled him back into his seat.

Linda grinned, her pink dress billowing out at the waist, a bright white bonnet tied around her head with a pink silk ribbon, and her black gumboots polished to a bright shine. Bonnet galloped along beside her and playfully nipped at her dress. The foal caught a bit of lace in her mouth and pulled backwards. Linda pulled back, but the filly wouldn't let go. They ended up in a game of tug-of-war. The crowd roared with laughter.

Ross ran over and grabbed Easter's lead line from his sister while Linda continued to fight to get the lacy bottom of her dress out of Bonnet's mouth. Bonnet finally let go and Linda fell backwards with a thump. She landed on the ground with her dress tucked up around her waist, her legs splayed out in the dirt and her gumboots facing toes up. She burst into a fit of giggles as Johnny and Hannah ran to help her to her feet. Bonnet leapt into the air, all four hooves off the ground. The naughty filly then trotted around to the far side of her mother, her eyes sparkling with mischief.

Cameras clicked and whirled.

Linda got up, a cheeky grin on her face. Her family and friends gathered around her. Easter snorted and nuzzled her master. Linda stroked the soft hairs on Easter's muzzle, while Hannah tried to brush the brown stain off the back of Linda's dress. Bonnet eye-balled Linda from underneath her mother's neck, then looked at the people in the yard as if sizing up her next victim.

"Maybe I better change her name to Twister," Linda groaned.

Her brother honked in amusement. Johnny chuckled and kept a wary eye on the little filly. Hannah laughed out loud.

"That might be a good idea," Ross whispered to his sister.

"Oh, you are a mess," Hannah added.

"I think we'll be talking about this day for a long time. It certainly has been an Easter to remember!" Pastor Smith howled.

The townsfolk stood up, clapping and hooting. Bonnet flicked her tail and ducked behind Easter. Easter moved her body sideways, blocking Bonnet from view.

Linda laughed and reached over to tickle the foal under its chin. Bonnet playfully nipped her fingers.

"Yes, it certainly is an Easter to remember," Linda agreed.

ℓ ⁴⁴⁻³